THE BREADOWN

Michael Warwick

<u>Disclaimer</u>

This book is a work of fiction. All names, characters, places and incidents in this story are either a product of the author's imagination or are used fictitiously. Any resemblance to the actual statements, opinions or actions of real people, living or dead, at past or existing locations is entirely coincidental.

1

Bartica, British Guiana 1955

The moon stared down at George as he stood, silent and motionless, watching the mighty Essequibo river flow relentlessly towards the Atlantic Ocean. After a minute or two of quiet contemplation he fumbled in his gabardine trousers and retrieved a packet of Marlborough cigarettes. With his other hand, he took out a silver Elgin lighter and lit a cigarette. Lost in his own thoughts he peered into the darkness, inhaled deeply and held the smoke in his lungs, for several seconds, until he forced it out of his nostrils and watched as it was sucked to the river by the cool night wind.

"Are you okay?"

George turned around abruptly and stared at the small figure holding an even smaller bundle between her arms. Silence ensued, save for the crashing of waters behind him.

"Yes, of course," he said as he looked intently into the dark brown eyes of Beebi. "Of course, I am. Sorry about this."

He held the cigarette between thumb and forefinger and smiled an inscrutable smile. With a flick of his thick wrist the cigarette landed on the water and floated, still alight, down the fast moving, dark river on its single journey to oblivion.

"I know I promised to give them up, but the hotel was offering them free as a promotional gimmick."

George pulled the white shawl covering the bundle Beebi was holding. He looked, lovingly, at the small baby fast asleep in the arms of his wife and then gently stroked his son's smooth, olive skinned cheek. The baby beamed sleepily, moved his head closer to his mother's breast and grabbed the gold necklace and pendant she was wearing. Both parents smiled and George placed his arm around his wife's slim waist and led her to a wooden bench facing the river.

"What were you thinking of?" enquired Beebi. "You seemed to be a million miles away."

"Just enjoying the view darling. We don't have such beautiful sights as these in Liverpool you know. The only time people go to the River Mersey is when they are emigrating not sightseeing," he replied seating his young wife on the bench.

"I'd love to travel to Liverpool one day," Beebi whispered looking at her son. "With you and Steven."

"Well one day maybe. I've still got to manage work in the coastal areas remember."

"Khartoon says London is lovely and the people are friendly... most of the time. Although she did say she doesn't like the winters because they are so cold," she said kissing her son's ruddy cheek.

"We'll see," replied George. "One step at a time. I'd like Steven to grow up and appreciate his home first. Which is British Guiana after all. He'll go to the best school here and have the best medical care. I'm not sure he'd get all those things in England unless I get my promotion. That's why I've got to get this job completed well."

"But you said we'd go to England after Steven was born," Beebi retorted sadly, rocking her son asleep.

There was silence. George watched the fireflies dancing about in the distance. The sight of the light from the fantastic creatures, pulsing on and off, synchronised with the beating of his heart. Slowly the rhythm of his heart grew faster and louder as the light from the tiny creatures grew brighter and bigger. He was mesmerized by nature's luminescent sprites and oblivious to all around him. Words from Beebi entering his consciousness had no meaning, the cool night breeze stroking his face left no impression and the murmur from the river circumvented his emotions. He was held hostage to the internal chemical circuitry of his brain which now had fused and left him impotent and powerless. His pupils dilated like a couple of blue balloons, beaded bubbles of sweat appeared around his temples and his body began to overheat.

"George, George, George!" Beebi shook her husband but to no avail. Seconds seemed like hours. She continued shaking him until Steven started to cry, awoken by the anxiety he could feel radiating from his mother.

"I'm okay," murmured George exiting from his petite mal. "I'm okay, just let me catch my breath."

George stumbled to his feet and held onto the side of the bench. He blinked several times to refocus his eyes and inhaled the cool, night air. Beebi watched anxiously. She had witnessed his temporary lapses of consciousness on several occasions before and each time she had worried herself sick. Not knowing what to do to help her husband ate away at her like a worm gnawing slowly through a rotten apple and each time she saw her husband incapacitated, in such a way, even for a few minutes, rendered her to bouts of creeping foreboding and hopelessness.

He was her anchor. But at times like this, she felt as if she had been cut adrift to sail, alone, along the sea of angst to a faraway abandoned land. If only he would listen and seek medical help. Then, at least, she would feel more secure in the knowledge that he was getting adequate treatment. But no! Her husband was too stubborn, like most of the Guianese men she had met.

"What's wrong with Steven?"

She looked at George and gripped his hand tightly.

"Your back. Oh God thank you," tears trickled down her cheeks and she pulled Steven closer to her face. "He's all right. He's just hungry. How are you feeling?"

"Fine. Why are you asking? You're always asking me the same thing. I'm okay," the venom in her husband's words left her feeling desolate and obsolete. "Sometimes I wish you'd leave me alone!" Suddenly a cold breeze wrapped itself around the family forming a fragile bond between husband and wife. Beebi buried her head in her son's chest and started to sob uncontrollably. George sat down, confused and disorientated, and stared blankly at his wife and son. It seemed like Vayu himself had descended to Earth, under the direction of Vishnu, to drive a wedge between the couple. After what seemed to be an eternity the breeze released itself from its prisoners and coursed its way towards the dark, moody river, searching for more victims. George turned away from his family and looked forlornly at the small moonlit village which stretched ahead and merged, imperceptibly, into the darkness of the coastal plain. At moments like this he felt alone, separate and disillusioned. He didn't know why or how his emotions kept on switching from one pole to another, but he knew that his mental condition was not only injurious to his well-being but also damaging to his family's welfare. But what could he do? Emotional Literacy had never been his strong point. Indeed, his mother would always comment, at the most inopportune or embarrassing moment, such as weddings, deaths and christenings that he was so much like his father. His father! The very thought of the man who would often beat and seldom spoke to him let alone embrace him, would stimulate an anxiety attack that would render him as helpless and speechless as a new- born baby. Indeed, he knew since he was a teenager that he had, unfortunately, inherited certain limiting, negative traits from his father, namely an unhealthy predisposition for solitude and the inability to communicate frankly with family, friends and foe alike. Even now, with his wife in tears, he could not walk across the bridge of emotions so that he could comfort her, hold her, rescue her from the depths of emotional despair she was feeling. No! He was immobilized by fear. Fear of not knowing what to say or do.

"We'd better get back to the hotel," he said as he rose and walked towards the hotel still slightly somnolent. "It's going to rain."

Beebi stood up and, still trembling and hurt by her husband's insensitive remarks, placed her left hand on his shoulder. He tensed but didn't move. She knew this reaction ever so well but left her hand on her partner and rested her head on his chest

"I love you," George knew Beebi's words were directed at him but said nothing. "I have always loved you. From the first time I saw you on your motorcycle on the plantation. You were so handsome. All my friends said to look out for the Englishman with the curly, fair hair, blue eyes, big chest and strong legs. You did look funny in those khaki shorts. But they were right. You were handsome. And, although I didn't tell them at the time, I promised myself that I would become your wife. And now I am."

She waited for a response, but none was forthcoming.

"I ..I...I." Beebi stopped. Tears rolled down her face. "I'll always love you. I just wish you'd let me in...let me into your world sometimes. I could help you. You know I want to help you."

George relaxed. He lifted part of the shawl, which had been blown off by the breeze, back onto his son's head. He turned and looked into his wife's eyes. He saw love and devotion, kindness and honesty and respect and truth burnt into her retina. However, the deeper he looked the more guilty he became because as he stared into her very id he also deciphered loneliness and despair, sadness and death.

"I know you do." he said and pulled Beebi closer towards him and kissed her on her lips in a clumsy attempt to appease her.

White-grey clouds slowly moved across the night sky disfiguring the hoary face of the moon. Suddenly, heavy raindrops began to fall in such torrents that it seemed that Artemis herself had decided to flood the land because her privacy had been invaded by natures ghosts. The heavy, warm droplets pummelled into George's face washing away the stupor he had been exposed to. His senses fully returned, he grabbed his wife's hand and they ran across the field back to their hotel.

2

Bookers, the English owners of the vast sugar plantations in British Guiana, had, by the late nineteen forties, monopolised the sugar industry in the colony. To many indigenous poor Guianese, especially of Indian and African descent, the company provided much needed employment for communities which had been impoverished before, during and after World War Two. To others, like Amir Khan, a lawyer with Marxist-Leninist ideals and a rising star in Guianese politics, and George Winwick, an expatriate Englishman seeking adventure and knowledge, the culture of slave and master could not have manifested itself more ignominiously than in the pernicious relationship that existed between Bookers, the dominant white owners of the sugar estates, and the passive black and brown cane-cutters and factory workers.

George, despite being part of the establishment, was viewed by friends and enemies alike as a maverick. Intelligent, witty, physically strong, handsome and liberal he was the embodiment of the typical Englishman. However, unlike his counterparts, he had despite his years in British Guiana felt uneasy with the trappings of the relative wealth and privileges he received because of his position of overseer of the Wales sugar plantation. At many company dinners, cricket lunches and beach parties he would defend the rights of the workers to form unions and argue for the improvement in working practices and living standards of the men and women he managed. To some colleagues he was a beloved, harmless Byronesque idealist but to others he was a dangerous, blinkered radical who would undermine the very regime that they adhered to and supported.

Nevertheless, George would often admonish friends and foe alike when they referred to the indentured Indians as coolies and Africans as niggers despite the fact, that to many managers, the need to use those derogatory terms of reference was seen as signs of strength and a means to demonstrate who held the power in the land of many rivers as British Guiana was fondly referred to.

"But George," urged Debbie. "If we did what you suggest then British Guiana would become like India... independent."

"What's wrong with that?" replied George wistfully. "It's their country. Shouldn't they own it? We can work in harmony with all of the communities."

"Schiss. Shit. Rubbish," bellowed Hans, a German who worked as an accountant and surveyor for Bookers. "If they get equality and independence this goddam country will revert back to what it was in the nineteenth century a malaria infested jungle."

Hans picked up a bottle of Bank's beer and downed it in one. He looked at George and smiled.

"You see this bottle," Hans lifted the empty bottle and shook it side to side. "It's empty. All the contents are gone. Do you know where they've gone? Do you? Yes, in me. And all that's left is the shell of a bottle. What can you do with that shell? Mr. High and Mighty. What? I'll tell you what. Nothing! You can't do anything with it. It's useless unless you want to piss in it."

Hans laughed. His huge frame convulsed and his blonde hair, wet with the heat of the day and waters from the sea, coursed over his eyes. His muscular hands swept the hair from his face and he stopped laughing. Staring directly at George he continued.

"You see, my English friend, British Guiana without me, you, Bookers is and always will be an empty shell. These niggers and coolies can't even blow their own noses without our help. How on earth can they run their own country?"

George said nothing. Hot not only from the midday sun but also from the anger he was feeling towards Hans, he stood up and smiled inscrutably.

"No sarcastic answer my friend? That's unlike you," continued Hans as he stood squarely in front of George.

The lapping of the waves as they ebbed and flowed up the baking hot golden beach, together with the Kiskadees, flying around the coastal margins whilst chattering, harshly and loudly, '*BEE-tee- WEE, BEE-tee-WEE, BEE-tee-WEE,*' were the sounds of nature which broke the unholy silence that pervaded the picnic area as the two adversaries stared at each other.

Hans stood motionless and menacing. He was the stereotypical Hitlerite member of the Aryan race. A former member of the Nazi Luftwaffe, who had witnessed dozens of his comrades killed by the English, he had developed an unhealthy pathological dislike of Englishmen and anything English.

"Your silence betrays your ignorance and cowardice, my English friend," Hans said threateningly tensing his body in anticipation of a fight.

The blood in George's vein began to boil, his heart started to beat faster and louder and he involuntarily began clenching his fists. Just before he was about to lunge at his German foe, a flock of pugnacious Kiskadees' swooped violently over Hans' head causing him to flail at his feathery attackers in a desperate and undignified manner forcing him to run ignominiously to the shelter of the coastal trees.

The group of friends laughed hysterically at the sight of the German slipping on the sand continuously as he tried to escape the beaks of the Kiskadees'.

"Erhalten Sie Weg. Erhalten Sie Weg. Erhalten Sie Weg," shouted Hans as he lunged for safety.

"I think that must be German for get away," sniggered Debbie to her friends.

George stood watching the comical spectacle played out before him and a rueful smile etched its way across his face. The tension flowing through his body moments before began to subside. He could feel his cortisone levels rebalance themselves and as he inhaled the salty air, he regained his senses and began walking towards his group of friends.

"Are you all right George? You shouldn't let him get to you. He's twisted," Debbie rose and faced George as she made the point.

Debbie had arrived in British Guiana on the same day as George. Married to the Dutch General Manager of Bookers, who was fifteen years her elder, she had struck up an immediate rapport with George as they sat next to each other on the Boeing 707. Intelligent, petite, auburn-haired with brown eyes she effused the charisma which opened doors wherever she went. Even though her marriage to Jan Kuiper De Witt was a marriage of convenience, as both were from families with impeccable aristocratic backgrounds, she did love him but found life in British Guiana an immense bore. She preferred the climate, art galleries and haute couture of Europe together with the social intercourse of traditional events and balls to the oppressive heat, lack of social events and the nouveau riche of her new country of residence. However, despite her misgivings, she had agreed to enjoy her stay in British Guiana and support her husband.

"I'm glad you didn't wallop him, George. I don't think Jan would have appreciated his financial whizz kid coming into the office with a black eye and broken hand."

A whimsical smile spread across George's face. He liked Debbie, not just because of her beauty but because of her incisive wit and charming intelligence. He also liked the fact that she exuded a dark sexuality which drove most red-blooded males insane. Indeed, he had noticed that whenever Debbie visited the sugar cane fields with her husband the workers would redouble their efforts, not to impress Mr. De Witt, but to gain his wife's attention by slashing the cane stalks at such a rate that they would often tire themselves out before the working day was completed.

"Don't worry. I had everything under control," he replied. "In any case I'm well aware of how close Hans and your husband are."

"Please George, don't go into that here. I'm on your side remember."

"I know. I know. I'm sorry!" He apologised.

A momentary silence ensued. He stared at Debbie and was about to continue when suddenly Hans appeared shaking sand off his bull-like chest.

"Schiis birds. If I had my gun with me, I'd blast them all out of the sky.

"If you had your gun you would have shot yourself." Debbie retorted sarcastically as she grinned mischievously at George.

On hearing the remark George bent double and deliberately let out a loud laugh knowing full well it would antagonise the German.

Hans humiliated and ridiculed turned to George and mouthed, "Next time Englishman. Next time."

3

In the backroom of a chandler's shop, situated in a small sleepy village named Uitvlugt, on the west bank of the Demerara river, a crowd of Indian and African men and women sat quietly. At the door which led into the shop two tall, muscular, Indian cane-workers stood guarding the entrance, machetes in hand. Suddenly, a dusty, black Morris Minor roared up to the building up and three distinguished Indian men and a beautiful, light-skinned Portuguese woman alighted and made their way into the building.

"Welcome Mr. Khan," said one of the cane-workers to the tallest of the three Indian men walking into the shop.

Mr. Khan smiled and shook the cane-workers hand who then shut and bolted the front door. Mr. Khan made his way to the front of the room and stood, imperiously, whilst his entourage sat on the row of wooden chairs facing the expectant crowd.

"I'm glad to see so many familiar faces and new ones," Mr. Khan exclaimed, staring directly at George. "As you know the British, working in secret with the American CIA, conspired, illegally I may add, to remove me, after one hundred and thirty-three days only, from power after a democratic, colonially administered election."

"Disgraceful," shouted a thin, toothless Indian cane- worker sitting in the front row. "Typical of the white slaveowners."

With those words a melee of indignation flew ferociously across the room with many men standing up gesticulating and venting their fury by ripping up the newspapers' they were carrying.

Mr. Khan stood watching the furore in mild amusement. He

turned and looked at his wife and winked at her. She remained calm and collected and pulled out a compact case from her Liberty bag and proceeded to dab her face with lavender scented powder.

Mr. Khan raised his arms above his head like a snake charmer and the nest of vipers in front of him fell silent, recoiled and sat back on their seats. Charisma and confidence radiated from Mr. Khan and those qualities, combined with his innate ability to persuade and influence, attracted supporters wherever he went. His power of rhetoric was so infectious that hundreds of his followers had openly promised that they would sacrifice their lives for him...a promise which had, unfortunately, been kept by five Indo-Guianese die-hard devotees who had been brutally gunned down by the police at Enmore some seven years earlier.

Mr. Khan raised his finger to his lips and silence ensued in the small, darkened room. "Comrades," he continued. "It is time we made this country ours. For far too long our voices have been ignored despite out right to articulate them. It is our right to voice our concerns and wishes. It is our right to have them heard and it is our right to have them considered."

A thunderous round of applause reverberated inside the room and shouts of Khan echoed throughout as if one was watching a cricket match.

Mr. Khan grinned imperiously and once again sneaked a look at his wife. She smiled back at him, knowing that her husband was in full control and at the height of his powers.

"Comrades, Comrades. As you know I use this term lightly and sarcastically in full view of the fact that I and yourselves have been accused of being communists," Khan paused and surveyed the room soaking in the atmosphere. "We the Guianese Peoples Party do not ally ourselves wholeheartedly to Communists, Marxists, Stalinists, Leninists, Moaists or any other ists if the truth be told." Again, a tsunami of approval cascaded amongst the congregation. "But indeed if we take some of their ideas and ideals to improve the lot of our people, to build better housing, to improve the health service, to provide a free education for all of our children and to give every citizen of this proud and beautiful land rights to live free from persecution, discrimination and starvation then yes, yes, yes indeed, I will be gladly be called a communist, but I'd rather be called a Guianaist!"

On hearing Khan's impassioned speech all the men and women in the room stood up, whistled and cheered and patted each other on the back. Khan sat down next to his wife and sipped some sweet coconut water which had been placed on the table by one of his aides. His wife, Isabella, the party's secretary squeezed his hand and whispered, "Well done my love. But be careful not to stir them up too much. You know what happened last time."

Khan smiled back and remembered the incident. Raymond Lloyd, a Socialist and the party's chairman, together with himself, had addressed a huge crowd of cane-workers on the Wales plantation site on a balmy Sunday evening, two weeks earlier, when word of the meeting had been scurrilously forwarded to the British Governor, who immediately ordered over one hundred policemen and soldiers to halt proceedings. However, due to Lloyd's vitriolic and powerful speech certain sections of the cane-workers, fuelled with local Demerara rum, had taken issue to the arrival of the police and soldiers and readily attacked them with machetes, knives, bamboo canes and guns. The ensuing fracas culminated in the soldiers turning their weapons on the cane-workers leaving over thirty men severely injured. Luckily, the leaders of the G.P.P. had been chaperoned into their cars, minutes earlier, and escaped unhurt.

"No. It will be all right. We've got lookouts for a mile or so," replied Khan as he sipped his drink, wiped the perspiration from his forehead and stood up to address the crowd once more.

"Sir Arthur Wilde. Yes, our beloved Governor," shouted Khan theatrically. "Sits in the Government House, Georgetown and eats the food our fellow workers produce with their blood, sweat and tears whilst hundreds of our brethren die daily from starvation and thousands more are malnourished and thousands more are homeless. Is this justice? Is this British justice? Is this God's justice?"

"No!" roared the excited crowd.

"Sir Arthur Wilde! Wilde by name and wild by deed. You all remember how he, with the backing of Her Majesty's Government, organized a coup d'etat against our party, suspended your civil rights and imprisoned many of you without cause and trial. He and his Government profess to have British Guiana's interest at heart. Why then didn't he accept the result of the elections? Democracy means accepting the will of the people, but Wilde wants the ruling party of British Guiana to be a reflection of his own British Government. As such he and his minions spread falsehoods about the G.P.P. He espouses that we are a communist organization hellbent on subverting the existing government and making British Guiana an ally of the Soviet Union...this is a gross untruth peddled by our enemies. Furthermore, Wilde asks us to let labour give its best because then, and only then will capital deal justly with its employees. What is he really intimating? What? What?"

"Tell us, tell us!" the crowd shouted ferociously inflamed by their leaders' passion and vitriol.

"I will tell you," Khan replied in a whisper. "He is saying you don't work to the best of your ability... you don't work hard enough."

"Nonsense!' screamed his followers.

"He thinks the scars on your back are the testimony to indolence rather than to blood, sweat and tears. He is a man bereft of conscience. He doesn't really care about the privation, malnutrition and unemployment you endure. He doesn't want you to organise and bargain through the trade unions of your own choice and to take part in the running of the industries in which you are engaged. Is it unfair for the working man to have a voice and have his rights upheld via trade unions? No. Wilde and his business friends... the newspaper owners, the sugar plantation owners, the Christian denominations who control our education system are the devils who are keeping us in the eighteenth century. We have to overthrow the system."

Clapping and shouts of approval echoed around the small room whilst many of the congregation chanted 'British out!' and 'Guiana for the Guianese'. However, a small, thin, moustached Indo-Guianese cane-worker sitting next to George stood up and cried out, "What should we do then?"

Khan motioned to the excited crowd to be silent. He smiled, looked piercingly into the cane-worker's eye and said, "By negotiation, my friend, by negotiation."

"Forgive me Mr. Khan," the man replied. "I'm not educated like yourself. I'm a simple man living a simple life. I work in the cane field from dawn to dusk and I provide for my wife and my family as best as I can. You say we have to negotiate to change things. But we have tried to negotiate ever since nineteen forty-eight and look where it has got us. We have to do more than negotiate. We have to send the British back to where they came from. Guiana is for the Guianese. We can run the country just like India is doing now."

An embarrassing silence ensued for a moment or two until Khan addressed the question.

"Inty?" Khan said to the man, "It is Inty, isn't it?"

Khan had crossed swords with Inty before in hustings and open meetings. Inty, although a cane-worker and uneducated was by no means unintelligent and his grasp of politics and his ability to argue his case coherently and logically had been noted by the higher echelons of the G.P.P. Khan, himself, knew the capabilities of Inty but saw a dark side which if unleashed could undermine the good work the party had recently made and cause a schism which would render the party redundant.

"Violence, my friend, leads to violence. Remember what Ghandi said? *An eye for an eye and the whole world would go blind.* And remember what happened at Enmore. We must argue our case. We must organize ourselves within the law and if the law fails us, we must seek to change the law. We want democracy not dictatorship! We want fairness not fighting! We want change with agreement not change with blood! We will persuade and we will reform. We will secure freedom and we will secure our future!"

"But what if they won't listen? What if they send in more soldiers from England to force their will upon us?" replied Inty.

"As you said yourself look at India. The British sent in more soldiers but in the end the political will of the people triumphed."

"Yes, but Independence didn't come without bloodshed so we have to consider an uprising."

"And who will fund the uprising? Who will you attract to join you in the uprising? I ask you not to go down this path of destruction. We are a country with only half a million people. How long do you think it will take for the British to crush an uprising as the one you are implying? No, my friend, negotiation and pressuring world opinion will win us our Independence."

Sweat dripped from Inty's brow. Pulsating neurons sped from his amygdala like bullets fired from an Uzi submachine gun. His heart began to beat fast and his mouth became drier. But suddenly, as if a switch had been pressed on his confusing thought of flight, freeze or fight mode his pre-frontal cortex kicked in enabling him to calm down, cool down and sit down. Rationality poured back into his thought process enabling him to realise this was not the time or place to harangue a politician of the calibre of Khan. Inty's dark gaze fell from Khan's stare, he shrugged his shoulders and remained silent.

"I think you have made a wise decision, my friend," Khan said looking around the crowd who stared solemnly at Inty waiting for a more aggressive response.

"We all know that, from reading the British newspapers and listening to the British radio, Wilde and the British politicians are feeding lies to our people and the rest of the world. And what are these lies, my friends? What are they?"

Khan stepped down from the makeshift stage and began to walk lion-like amongst the crowd. Slowly, imperiously, confidently Khan looked into the eyes of his spell-bound audience and stopped in front of George. Smiling he whispered, "What are they?"

George sat quietly and unmoved by Khan's stare or question. He looked at the politician and ruminated that this man was, indeed, a man of conviction, of intellect and of power.

Khan turned abruptly from George and with a gigantic leap he once more stood on the stage and exclaimed in a mighty voice, the tone of which made his wife drop her compact case onto the wooden floor. "What are they? Well, my friends they have connived to convince the good people of England and the rest of the world that we, the G.P.P, in this colony want to set up a one-party state, a police state and a Communist state. But what aren't they telling everyone? What? They are not telling the world that in British Guiana there is land hunger. Yes, land hunger! The white sugar plantation owners do not want us to cultivate the vast acres of land for rice. No. They want the workers to stay on the sugar plantations so the price of rice can be kept low. They do not want competition lest the price of rice rose and became more profitable than sugar production. They do not want factories or industries set up otherwise workers will move to these new places of work and earn more money. So, you see, my friends, we have to work together to redress the situation and force these transgressors to tell the truth to the world. The world must know that we are not communists. They must know that we are a democracy whose life is slowly being extinguished by the capitalist sugar plantation owners working hand in glove with the English Motherland. The British do not want our Indian and African brethren to escape from the plantations like our Portuguese and Chinese brothers did, otherwise what would happen to their profits? No, my friends we must work together, and within the law to gain our economic and social freedom."

4

Bookers' management board members sat around an immense, oval satinwood table adorned with vintage silver cutlery and cut- glass decanters and wine glasses. The room was expansive with all walls decorated with framed photographs of Queen Elizabeth the Second and antique maps of British Guiana. Two huge wooden fans, hanging from the ceiling, slowly revolved transmogrifying the warm air into cool air. At the head of the table sat the Director of the company Mr. De Witt. Next to the Director sat Hans wearing a cream coloured linen jacket, too tight at the midriff, a white shirt and a blue Booker embossed logo tie with a gold Luftwaffe tie pin attached to it. To the right of Mr. De Witt sat Ali Persaud, the newly appointed Deputy Manager of the Wales plantation and to his right sat a disinterested George. A further three white managers sat opposite George and Ali Persaud. Just behind De Witt stood two Indian servants wearing white gloves, starched white shirts with black ties and black trousers. They stood motionless, like the sphinxes of Giza, staring, as if hypnotized, at the fans.

"Welcome to this meeting gentlemen," De Witt said in a quiet, unassuming, but assured voice whilst making eye contact with each, and every one of his management team. Light from the mid-day sun streamed into the room and reflected off his horn-rimmed glasses casting a spot of bouncing light ricocheting of the walls as he turned and faced his team.

"As you are aware, reasonable progress is being made in the expansion of our company. However, after my tete- a -tete with Mr. Hans Schelling, our esteemed financial gatekeeper, there are some anomalies regarding costings which we will have to investigate further in order that our targets, present and future, are to be met."

At the mention of Hans, George let out a restrained cough and his wooden chair screeched against the wooden floor like a banshee screaming in the darkness of the night. All eyes fell onto George.

"Are you all right Mr. Winwick?" enquired De Witt.

George motioned with a nod that he was and took out a white handkerchief from his blue, blazer pocket to contain his coughing fit. Hans stared at him, malevolently.

De Witt clicked his fingers and an Indian servant quickly walked to George's side, leaned across the table and poured him a glass of red wine from a crystal decanter.

George took a sip and thanked the servant.

"I'm okay."

"As I was saying. Finances must be at the forefront of our minds whatever project we are completing otherwise we will have, as the English say, a monkey on our backs who will drag us down. I'll pass you to Hans who will suggest some strategies which will help us to get back on the right financial track."

De Witt sat down, took off his glasses, blew nonchalantly onto both lenses and wiped them with his linen table napkin.

"First of all," Hans, still languishing in his chair and staring directly at George, boomed across the room. "We must eliminate waste!" George diverted his gaze to a droplet of red wine floating on the napkin underneath the glass the servant had handed to him. He raised his index finger and nudged it. The upper part of the droplet moved but remained intact and quickly regained its former shape. George, annoyed, nudged the droplet again but exerted a slightly greater force. Once again, the upper part of the droplet moved but the rest of its body remained stubbornly glued to the napkin. George took aim at the droplet once more but instead of just nudging the bubble of wine he flicked it so hard, like a monstrous Dickensian teacher flicking the ear of poor unfortunate pupil caught misbehaving, the droplet burst into myriads of tinier globules landing in the middle of the table.

"Waste Is everywhere," continued Hans, raising his voice in anger at George's deliberate act of disrespect. "From the ordering, accidentally, ignorantly or fraudulently of materials not needed for a particular job, to the acceptance by managers, at all levels of the service, of overlooking the niggers and coolies not working to their full capacity."

The assembly of managers listened intently to Hans tirade and although some, such as Ali Persaud, gave Hans a disapproving look at the racialist language being used, none were prepared to launch an objection on the grounds that they knew that whatever Hans said was to a great extent supported by De Witt.

"Waste has to be eliminated...." Hans stopped as his speech was interrupted.

"Excuse me. But what did you just say?" George said as he stared at Hans. "What did you say? I wasn't listening."

Hans sat silently in anger as the vein at the side of his temple began to pulsate quickly. Seconds flew by.

"We must eliminate waste." retorted Hans

"No, not that part."

Hans stood up, violently, from his chair.

"Not that part. Not that part. Which part are you gibbering on about you buffoon?"

"The part before the waste," George replied calmly.

"What? Niggers and coolies. That part?"

George rose from his chair slowly and deliberately. He stood facing Hans squarely but looked in De Witt's direction.

"Yes, that part."

"Why what's wrong with niggers and coolies? A good manager uses these words to ensure they get these ignorant, illiterate, bastards to do the work on time and in a good way. Do you have a problem with that?"

"Not only do I have problem with that. I have a problem with you. These niggers and coolies, as you put it, are human beings and should be treated as such and accorded the respect any gentleman would endeavour to afford another gentleman. Without them, Bookers wouldn't have a bank account worth millions of dollars. You offend me and I object, in the strongest terms possible, the use of these derogatory terms. Who do you think you are?"

"Mein Gott Du Indischer liebhaber. Du bist ein Arsch."

Hans thumped the table with his hand. The force from the strike toppled over several wine glasses drenching the table in red wine staining the white linen tablecloth.

"Now Hans," De Witt said calmly mopping up a pool of burgundy with his napkin. "Don't rise to the bait. If you want to reply to George's cogent statement do so. But with composure and decorum."

"I am," Hans paused staring at George directly. "The man who has to balance the books. The man who has to ensure that mistakes made in the field by so called managers and overseers, like you, are rectified in order that the company can send a profit margin back to head office in England. In other words, I am your safety blanket. I am your security."

Hans sat down. The other board members waited for George to reply but he stood motionless still looking at the German. After a while George sat down, smiled and said, "I would rather try my luck with the prospectors on the Amazon panning for gold than relying on your expertise. I know who I'd sooner trust!"

Ali Persaud let out stifled guffaw and had to hold his napkin close to his mouth for fear of laughing out aloud at George's last remark.

Hans glanced blackly at his co-manager who rose and excused himself from the room.

"Touche, George," smiled De Witt. "But I'm sure you'd agree that our goal is for harmony amongst our managers otherwise the chain of command from the top to the bottom will collapse and with it our capacity to operate a finely tuned, workable organisation. In other words, one faulty cog will fracture the machine and without the machine we will be product less."

was the right man for the job and more importantly, he had been his close friend for several years.

"An interesting proposition Hans," commented De Witt looking at Ali. "But I will not sack any manager or overseer of mine on hearsay and innuendo. If George fails in his duties and it is proven that he is indeed, as you suggest, a supporter of Khan's, whose intention it is to undermine Bookers position in this area of the Caribbean, then I will give it some serious thought. We will see if he has changed his views after he completes the course, you suggest he undertakes, in England. That will give him ten months of reflection and contemplation. A good idea Hans. Gentlemen I formally call this meeting to an end."

5

The ramshackle wooden hut, which masqueraded as a home, was typical of dwellings constructed on the Uitvlugt estate or "the nigger yard" which the white plantation owners fondly referred them to at dinner parties. With a rusted, weather- beaten tin roof, woodworm ridden staircase, broken door and windows devoid of glass the hut was in a dilapidated, dire condition. George tapped on the door. There was no answer. He tapped again. Still no answer. He moved to one of the side openings and was about to peer through the rag material which acted as a curtain when he suddenly felt his left foot falling through a plank of wood.

"Big tree fall down, goat bite de leaf."

George looked around but couldn't see anyone. He moved the rag material and peered into the dark interior of the house. It was empty.

"If yuh eye nah see, yuh mouth nah must talk."

George, this time, pinpointed the direction of the voice. It was coming from the side of the hut.

"Aroun er man."

George turned and proceeded to walk carefully in the direction of the voice. As he reached the corner, he could see a sunny overgrown back yard. Two trees stood proudly in the yard, a mango tree heavily laden with ripe, reddish green succulent mangoes and a gynip tree whose branches were burdened with scores of green, oval- shaped fruit ready to eat. Between the two fruit trees hung a hammock made from canvas. The hammock bulged, slightly, in the middle and swung slowly from left to right.

"Wha yuh want Mr. George?"

George walked over to the voice clambering through the overgrown vegetation. The sulphurous smell from the wooden latrine, which stood awkwardly, directly behind the hammock caught his breath. George inhaled deeply.

"Never yuh mind de smell. Yuh get used to it man."

George looked at Inty. Inty was indeed an intriguing man. Thin but muscular, George stared at Inty's rope-like arms and legs. The man was certainly fit and handsome. He had high cheekbones, small, jet coloured eyes and a pencil thin moustache which reminded him of Errol Flynn. His black hair was brylcreamed and brushed back revealing a high, wrinkle-less forehead and his overall appearance conveyed to a stranger, a man in his twenties rather than the actual thirty-nine years he had lived boy and man on the sugar plantation.

"Yuh comin to check up on me Mr. George?"

George paused for a moment and then rested on the mango tree trunk. He took out his cigarette holder and offered a cigarette to Inty.

"You were quite impressive at that meeting at Uitvlugt. I'm intrigued by the fact that you can address a meeting via the Queen's English and revert back to pidgin. I thought you didn't go to school," said George.

Inty stopped rocking on the hammock and smiled, nonchalantly, at his friend revealing a fine set of white teeth.

"Me go to no school. Me to poor. But…"

Inty pointed to a transistor radio underneath his hammock.

"That is where, Mr. George, me learn yuh Queen's English. Me a chameleon. Me a leopard. Me whoever yuh want me to be Mr. George. Orange yellow but yuh nah know if he sweet."

"Point taken Inty and well put. But no. I'm not here checking up on you. I'm here to see how I can help to improve things."

Inty inhaled his cigarette and held the smoke within his mouth for a few seconds. Cheeks bulging, he slowly exhaled small, regular cloud circles into the air.

"Yeah man. Yuh Mr. George is a gentleman in the truest sense of de word. Yuh know de difference between right and wrong. Respect. Big respect to yuh! But...."

Inty stopped swinging in the hammock, swung his thin, wiry legs over and stared deeply into George's blue eyes.

"But yuh be careful Mr. George be careful. Yuh mean well. When coconut fall from tree he can't fasten back. Yuh understand what me mean Mr.George?"

"I'm not too sure Inty."

"Listen Mr. George. If me was yuh, me would take Beebi and yuh pickaninny and go back home. Back home to England were yuh be safe. British Guiana is now a dangerous place...a murderous place...."

Inty looked imploringly into George's eyes and knew that he would be a tremendous ally in the fight for independence in terms of intelligence, connections and resources. However, the very thought that George could be potentially killed defending the rights of the workers caused him much pain as George, in the years residing in the land of three rivers, had already given so much to Bookers and the Indians and Africans. Should he offer the ultimate sacrifice when so many British Guianese were quite happy to remain indifferent, insensitive and ignorant?

"Yuh would help us more in our fight against repression and exploitation by shipping out to Old Blighty and persuading de English politicians and Queen Elizabeth dat injustices are happening in dis beautiful country."

George said nothing but pondered Inty's words.

"British Guiana is going to explode Mr. George. Yuh know it and me know it and dis hammock know it," Inty said and both he and George began to laugh.

"When it explodes de bang will be carried by de hurricane all de way to Queen Elizabeth and knock her crown off."

George stifled a giggle and took a puff on his Marlborough cigarette. Since visiting Inty for the past two months he had enjoyed their evenings conversations because they provided him with a mixture of seriousness and humour which created a period of time, whereupon he could relax and muse upon the stresses of the days' work.

"But more seriously Mr. George, me don't want yuh or yuh family to get hurt. Yuh know der are spies everywhere."

George indeed did know that for a few dollars many Indian and African workers were willing to act as Quislings and convey to the Police or Bookers management confidential discussions which often led to murders and mutilations.

"*If I would fight for my liberty why wouldn't I fight for yours?* Do you remember this quote Inty? *If you will not fight for the right when you can easily win without bloodshed; if you will not fight when your victory will be sure and not too costly; you may come to the moment when you will have to fight with all the odds against you and only a small chance of survival. There may even be a worse case, you may have to fight when there is no hope of victory, because it is better to perish than to live as slaves*."

Inty stood up and threw his cigarette unto the floor. With his bare, calloused foot he extinguished the light. He grinned, stepped forward and hugged George.

After several seconds Inty extricated himself from his friend and tears welled up in his eyes.

"Yes Mr. George. Me remember yuh Mr. Winston Churchill speech. Me remember it."

"You see Inty my destiny for the time being is here. Whatever will be, will be. I am damned if I see my child grow up in a country full of slaves."

"Respect, Mr. George, big respect."

"You see Inty I could do both. I can let trade unionists, politicians and managers understand the plight that the Guianese are facing by letter and phone-calls without having to leave and more importantly I can serve the cause better by frequenting meetings held by the ruling elite and Bookers."

"But what about yuh and Beebi?"

"What do you mean Inty?"

"Mr. George, don't yuh think dat dey won't trust yuh because yuh go with a coolie woman?"

"Possibly Inty. In truth that is a possibility, but conscience makes cowards of us all. And I intend not to let conscience, in this instance, be my nemesis."

"Well Mr. George. If yuh really, truly are prepared for all eventualities, me know our organisation will welcome yuh services."

Inty beckoned his friend to follow him to the front of his house. Crossing the threshold into the interior of the building George noticed the absence of furniture save for an old stool and mattress strewn across the floor. Opposite the mattress, underneath a small window opening, a tin bucket served as a sink and next to it was a small table with a kerosene lamp on top. Inty walked to the lamp and lit it.

"Mr. George, many of yuh fellow managers and European workers think dat we, de working Guianese, de coolies and niggers...."

At these words George turned away from Inty and grimaced.

"Me know yuh don't use dose words, Mr. George. Me know. But yuh Booker people do. And dey use dem because dey think we are like donkeys, mules, dogs dat are to be treated in any way whatsoever. Dey don't see us, like yuh do, as human beings ...not even from de very first day me forefathers left India and travelled across de seas to work dese lands as indentured workers. We didn't come here as slaves like de Africans, but we are treated worse dan our African brothers."

George listened intently

"Mr. George yuh may not like de way we be treated by our masters but dat is not enough."

"But what else do I need to know Inty?"

"Yuh must feel de way we've been treated Mr. George. Yuh must feel de kiss of de whip as we cut de cane when de overseers say we work too slow. Yuh must taste de salt blood when we accidentally slash our limbs and our forced to work on without medication."

George remained silent

"Yuh see Mr. George, don't mind how bird vex, it can't vex

with tree. We will remain slaves for anuda one hundred years. No anuda thousand years if me people don't rise up and strike at de heart of our European masters...de economy. If we withdraw our labour dey get no money. If dey get no money dey go home. Me would rather starve more dan feed dem less."

Inty stood up and walked towards his bed. He bent forward looking for something and as he did his moth-eaten vest scrambled up his back, revealing whip scars etched on his upper buttocks. George stared at the marks until Inty turned around and lifted a green, battered suitcase onto his sheet-less, metal bed. He opened the suitcase and pulled out a bundle of letters tied with a red silk ribbon. George watched as he carefully untied the ribbon, lay it neatly adjacent to the case and removed a creased letter from a sallow envelope.

"Yuh read dis Mr. George."

"Are you sure Inty?" declared George hesitantly. "It is private after all."

"Me know. But it'll show yuh what me family go thru to get 'ere. Live 'ere and die 'ere. To lose der family. To lose der identity."

George slowly unravelled the letter fearing that he would rip one of the creases. The first thing he noticed about the letter's author was the pristine, cursive handwriting which flowed across the page.

"Me great, grandfather's son became a teacher in Calcutta. Yuh like de writing?"

"It's beautiful."

"Please Mr. George read de letter aloud."

George cleared his throat and began reading.

"Dear Respected Father.

I hope this letter finds you in good health. It is over seven years since I set eyes on you. I am now eleven years old my father, Father I am sorry to be the bearer of bad news. Your beloved sister, Amina, is now blind and destitute and I work in the fields all day and night to look after her and my mother, your wife. Things are really hard for us, my father, the money I earn is not enough to feed us. Many times we have no food to eat and now the monsoons are upon us"

George, welling up with emotion wiped a tear from his eye.

"Please Mr. George, please continue."

"Whenever you write your letters' I wish I was a bird and could fly to you. To see you my father. I have some more bad news my father. Your wife, my loving mother, is now very sick ...she might not live long. She keeps on crying to see you one last time, Please Father can you come back and be with us.

Your loving son, Abdul "

George stopped reading the letter and stared at the teardrops which had dripped from his eye and landed on the yellowed paper. Slowly the ink spread across the page blurring the words into a pattern of dark blue spots.

"Sorry Inty I ...I..."

"Don't yuh worry yuhself Mr. George," said Inty taking the letter and replacing it in the envelope. "It's only paper and ink. De words are locked in me mind forever like a caged lion. Whenever me want, me can let dat lion out so it can taste de air of freedom. Dat's when me remember de words, de sentences, de paragraphs of love and despair my ancestor wrote. Me never forget dose words Mr. George. Never!"

6

It was unusual for the Kiskadees' to be silent and even absent from the beaches in the late afternoon. To the village fishermen of Lake Mainstay, situated near the Atlantic coast, northwest of the mouth of the Essequibo river, the only times the noisy birds disappeared from the area occurred when the hurricane season hit the Caribbean or when the white plantation managers enjoyed an alcoholic bird shooting expedition, usually on a Sunday afternoon.

Beebi sat underneath a palm tree, shaded from the heat of the afternoon sun. Beside her in a white shawl lay Steven fast asleep holding a red rattle in his left hand. Beebi sang softly to her young son and gently stroked his forehead to soothe him whilst listening to the small, white horse waves lapping onto the shore. Looking at her son she felt immensely proud with herself. This was indeed why she had been born. To bring into the world a boy who would grow into a man, who would marry, be happy, have his own family and continue the life cycle that Allah had prescribed. Yes, she was indeed blessed. Her prayers had been answered and at this moment in time nothing, absolutely nothing could puncture her bubble of happiness. She closed her eyes for a moment as a cool breeze caressed her face and together with the shade of the palm tree she slowly leaned towards her baby and lay down fast asleep.

Away in the distance a small, dark Shadow prowled menacingly along the beach. The Shadow grew longer and longer as the sun slowly crawled across the light blue, cloudless sky. In the wake of the Shadow, at intervals of twenty feet or so, empty miniature bottles of Remy Martin cognac lay strewn in the sand leaving behind a snake like trail. As the Shadow neared Beebi, Steven's red rattle began to move slowly, by the breath of the breeze, making a rattlesnake sound which was oblivious to his mother. Finally, the Shadow reached his victims and malevolently hovered over them inhaling the scent of their bodies. Still Beebi slept, even though Steven began to kick and move his arms as if trying to find the light of the sun.

Suddenly from across the lake the wailing of the Kiskadees' could be heard. The sky became peppered with the large birds as they flapped furiously to the palm trees where the Shadow was enveloping Beebi.

As if from a waking dream Beebi heard a mixture of sounds-rattle, Kiskadees' and heavy breathing and she could see, blurrily, a combination of darkness and light as if she had experienced sunstroke. She tried to get up, but a heavy weight pushed down on top of her forcing her to sink further into the soft sand. She tried to raise herself again, but the dream wouldn't end, and she felt even more immobile. She opened her eyes slightly and saw Steven with a disturbed look on his face. She heard his rattle getting louder and louder and louder. She turned her head to see what was pinning her down but as she did so, darkness descended as if curtains had been drawn across a window, The Shadow had covered her face and was making an ungodly noise. Unexpectedly she felt a sharp, burning sensation in her vagina. This was not a dream. She tried to stand up again but despite her heroic efforts she could not shift the weight of the Shadow. The more she resisted the more the Shadow seemed to get immense pleasure from violating her. She cried for help, but her screams were stifled by the Shadow. Time froze. Beebi prayed for help and within a few seconds Allah had granted her wishes as she extricated her hand from the grip of the Shadow and grabbed hold of her son's arm in order to protect him. Nevertheless, the Shadow still hung over her like a dark brooding cloud ready to jettison its watery load. Slowly, the Shadow began to change shape and Beebi began to breathe more freely. The Shadow grew smaller and smaller and smaller. Beebi felt as if she could open her eyes knowing that her attacker had satiated itself and she was safe. After what seemed an eternity, she decided to raise herself off the ground. But just as her eyelids began to open completely the shadow returned. Beebi grimaced, closed her eyes again and let out a stifled scream. Surprisingly, the shadow echoed her scream. She was confused. The shadow's voice seemed familiar. Why was it shouting her name? Why was it now seeming concerned about her welfare? Was it a ploy? Was the shadow playing an ugly game? Did the shadow want to place her in a position of false security? To give her hope then only to dash it! Why? Why?

"Beebi. Beebi!"

The shadow was to Beebi as the Harpyes were to King Phineus. But who would be her Jason? Beebi, despite her pain, recalled the story of Jason and the argonauts being told by her teacher, Mr. Ali, in her last year of an interrupted school life when she was nine years old. She had loved listening to the Greek myths and the way Mr. Ali had brought them to life via his acting techniques and she had committed them to memory. Now in her hour of need which of the gods and goddesses would rescue her? Which? She could not see her future unlike Phineus who could see his. All she could see was darkness. All she could feel was emptiness. All she could hear was the shadow calling her name in an imploring manner.

"Beebi, Beebi! Can you hear me? Can you hear me? You are safe now."

Beebi opened her eyes.

"Beebi, Beebi! Are you okay?"

She didn't want to look at the shadow, but an involuntary movement of her eyelids forced her to capture the image of the voice that was whispering to her. Through the haziness she could see a dark form appear. The shadow was shape shifting.

"Please not again. Not again. Not again," she pleaded in terror. And suddenly the Kiskadees', mimicking her tortuous screams, launched themselves into the air fleeing from the crime-scene.

As the birds' flapped away in a delta formation Beebi felt her son's arms flapping against her face as if he too was trying to escape the predicament himself.

"Don't hurt me again. Please leave us alone!"

Suddenly, the shadow spoke again and with it flooded back memories of love and safety not hatred and danger. Slowly the fog of pain cleared from her mind and she stretched out her hand to touch the shadow's visage. This time the shadow did not flinch and move away but rather let the hand caress its face. Beebi let out a stifled cry.

"Khartoon!"

"Yes, it's me Beebi. Lay still. Everything is going to be ok. I'll help you. Just don't move"

7

Mr. De Witt sat at the Governor's office table staring out of the window. Grey clouds drifted by, heavy and ponderous, like a herd of elephants walking across the savannah plains of Africa. The midday sun tried, forlornly, to peer from behind the leaden clouds but the herd closed in to block its view. Darkness pervaded the town centre and De Witt scanned the road below and watched the market traders frantically covering their wares in anticipation of the impending rains. He sipped the coffee he was holding and then took a long drag from the panatella he held in his right hand. He bent his head backwards and slowly blew several smoke circles into the air and watched as they were dispersed by the ceiling fan.

"So, what do you think?"

De Witt ignored the question. He inhaled deeply once more from his panatella, blew the smoke onto the window and stared at the round misty circle he had just formed on the glass surface.

"Believe me. If we don't sort this out, all hell will break loose."

The circle began to fade away. De Witt turned, stood up and looked at the men sitting around the table.

"Are you familiar with the philosopher Albert Camus?" De Witt said as he looked at Hans, Raymond Lloyd and Sir Arthur Wilde. "With regards your question Hans. Interesting as it may be, Camus said *revolt and revolution both wind up at the same crossroads, the police, or folly!* It may sound anodyne, but in my view, there is a grain of truth. Now we have the police, and soldiers I may add, but are we moving into the area of folly?"

Hans smiled and replied, "We can all philosophise Herr Witt.

Indeed, to paraphrase a hero of mine, mein Fuhrer Adolf Hitler, *for the greatest revolutionary changes on earth would not have been thinkable if their motive force was merely the bourgeois virtues of law and order.* Law and order have to be deconstructed in order that capitalism and dictatorship can move in and people like us rule and prosper."

A long pause ensued as De Witt, Raymond Lloyd and Sir Arthur Wilde gazed at one another. Raymond Lloyd cleared his throat and said indignantly, "As a moderate politician I cannot and will not subscribe to your views Hans. My belief systems are diametrically opposite to yours. Indeed, the Guianese Peoples Party won the election not because it wanted a dictatorship and capitalism but on the contrary because they knew the people wanted better living conditions and the right to strike which is part and parcel of universal suffrage and democracy."

"Yes. And look what is happening. We have riots. We have murders. We have the workers demanding higher wages and fewer working hours. What will this mean?" Hans said as he banged the table with both of his hands. "It will mean smaller profits. It will mean contraction of labour not expansion. It will mean less money in the economy and therefore British Guianas's infrastructure will jack-knife. It will mean they will want more unions. It will mean they will want independence!"

"And what is wrong with that?" Lloyd retorted sardonically.

"If I may interject," said Sir Arthur Wilde. "You are all too well versed with British politics Mr. Lloyd, especially after your studies in London. And you, as well as everyone else around this table, understand that independence, in the long term, is an inevitability, despite what the powers that be may say to the rest of the world. However, in the meantime the British Government will do everything in its power to maintain the status quo to protect its interests and ensure Communism in all its forms is extinguished in this colony. Furthermore, the British Government will champion British Guiana's desire for independence if and only if they agree to our plans which have been presented to the G.P.P."

Lloyd glared at Wilde and said, "You all know that Amir Khan and I were close allies and you are all well aware of the British Government's deliberate attempts to sabotage our recent visit to England."

Lloyd paused and looked at each of the men squarely in their eyes.

"Yes. I know how the political machine works. But it's a pity your Government does not train your people well enough in the art of counter espionage."

Wilde peered at De Witt and Hans.

"Yes, Amir Khan and I both knew of the plots to stop the airlines from selling us tickets so we could not enter England. And we knew about the bribing of our brother politicians in neighbouring islands. But didn't you think we had our own spies? How naïve. How do you think we eventually chartered an aeroplane to fly to England, to gain entry, to voice our woes to your people and to gain an audience with your very own Queen Elizabeth?"

The three men stared at Lloyd in silence.

"What no retort? No answers?" Lloyd rose from his seat and walked over to Hans and stood behind him holding the back of his chair with both hands.

"You see gentlemen not only do I have connections in England because of my University background, but I have influence, like Khan, with every part of the Guianese establishment."

"What are you intimating?" Wilde enquired curiously.

"I am intimating my dear Sir Arthur Wilde that you shouldn't trust anyone. Not even your closest ally in British Guiana. All is smoke and mirrors and believe me we know how to break mirrors and clear smoke."

"And we know how to rebuild them," interjected Hans thrusting his chair backwards forcing Lloyd to release his grasp from the top rail. "Do not be foolhardy in thinking we do not know how the schism between you and Khan could be, if Sir Arthur Wilde and his connections put their mind to it, further increased and therefore thwart your political ambition."

"Mr. Lloyd," added Sir Arthur Wilde. "I and the British Government are fully aware of your brilliant mind and your power of oratory."

Wilde rose from his chair and walked over to a Chippendale bureau, pulled open one of its ornate drawers and removed a bundle of papers from a manilla folder. He returned to the table were Lloyd stood and lay the bundle in front of him.

"You may have spies Mr. Lloyd but, as you know, politics is a cat and mouse game. And in these papers is your life story."

"You didn't need to convince me that you had a dossier on me Sir Arthur. I am fully aware of the processes Governments employ when seeking information about potential threats. Indeed, I know, from my mother, that correspondences I sent her from London had been intercepted and opened."

"Just as well Mr. Lloyd," continued Wilde. "We know all about your involvement in student politics and your belief in self-rule via the League of Coloured People. We also know that despite your previous allegiances with Khan and the G.P.P. you actually despise the thought of the Indians being in power.......so much for Guiana being for the Guianese...."

"More like Guiana being for the Africans." laughed Hans.

"As I was saying," Wilde said glaring at Hans. "Why, despite being leader of the British Guiana Labour Union, didn't you win the election to be G.P.P. leader? Do you think it was just due to the oratory of your arch- rival Stephen Queen or do you think maybe, just maybe the British had somehow infiltrated your union and the G.P.P. with Indian and African moles? Furthermore, whom do you think saved you from imprisonment when Khan and the rest of the G.P.P. were incarcerated? Whom?"

Lloyd stood stoically facing his adversaries.

"Yes, we do know what you and a thousand like you do. We have too for the sake of the continuing stability of this great country. We can't stand by idly and see it regress to the days of pre- colonialism."

"That is why," De Witt interrupted, looking at Lloyd and

Wilde. "It is important that we all sing from the same hymn sheet. We might not like the hymns but at least we know the words."

"I understand," said Lloyd. "But what do you expect me to do?"

De Witt walked over and stood by Hans.

"Sir Arthur Wilde and Bookers have held secret meetings, with the blessing of the British Government and selective personnel, such as Hans and have agreed on a course of action which will be of mutual benefit to yourself, Bookers and Great Britain."

"Communism, in the form Khan espouses," exclaimed Wilde. "Is anathema to Britain and yourself. As such I'm sure, with the help of the people that work for us, we could arrange for you to defeat Khan in the forthcoming G.P.P. elections and therefore plan the future of British Guiana in the way you see fit. However..."

"However?" interjected Lloyd. "You want the status quo regarding Booker's monopoly to remain and you want the British influence in the area maintained."

Wilde tapped on the bundle of papers with his index finger and shoved them in the direction of Lloyd. Lloyd stood for a few seconds motionless. He stared angrily at Wilde and the vein on the side of his neck began to pulsate like a car's piston. Suddenly he picked up the paper bundle and walked out of the room.

8

The small wooden church in Uitvlugt was packed with cane-workers, who sat solemnly listening to Khan. The impromptu meeting had been hastily convened on the back of the news that more Indians had been brutally murdered by negroes, at the behest, some had said, of Lloyd's henchmen. Kick down door and choke and rob were the hallmarks of those nefarious, bloody crimes with machetes being the negroes preferred weapon of choice. Also, the news that plans were afoot to hold elections sooner rather than later and that a rival party, founded by Lloyd, was about to challenge the G.P.P. had spearheaded Khan in organizing meetings across the country. He knew that a division between the rural, agricultural Indians and urban coastal negroes had been established since the 1940's but the situation had been exacerbated by the political machinations of the British government and the racist attitude of the negroes.

"Friends, comrades. We know the history of our country. We know all about our ancestors' trials and tribulations. Have things improved for us?"

"No," shouted a few men from the back of the room.

"Although we have a supposed allegiance with Lloyd, just look around this sacred room and count how many of our negro brethren have joined us for this meeting. Division exists between the foreigners and Guianese, Negroes and Indians. We must address this situation if we are to succeed in our attempts to unify our nation."

Numerous Indians shouted their approval on hearing Khan's

words but the few negroes attending the meeting sat stony faced and silent.

"Yes, the white man may have stopped trying to convert the Hindus to Christianity...stopped trying to feed them beef and the Mohammedans pork but nevertheless we are still slaves. The white expatriate managers still act as czars, kings, prosecutors and judges all in one. They live in massive, luxurious mansions and their overseers reside in their own segregated areas on the plantations, whilst the impoverished workers live in a hovel not fit for animals let alone humans."

Khan looked at his wife who sat on the front row pews surrounded by bodyguards and George. She smiled and nodded appreciatively. George mused that here indeed he was listening to a man whose charisma, presence and oratory skills would one day lead him to become a world leader.

"You know my friends," continued Khan. "Our forefathers told us, by the light of the kerosene lamps, stories of how the scheming Arkatis, in Damru Tapu, would spin their evil tales of easy money, to our ancestors in India. It's not surprising that our great grandparents from Bengal to Madras decided to take up the offer of a better life in these lands because theirs had been devastated and decimated by the British. What option did they have? Starve in their homeland or eat in a foreign land? My friends the British are repeating history here."

"Seven years nah too much fuh wash speck off bird neck," shouted a burly Indian from the middle of the room. Khan smiled and looked at the man. "Yes comrade. Yes! History does indeed tell us that some people will never ever change their ways and attitudes."

He took his white linen jacket off and placed it over the chair which stood behind him.

"Listen my friends. They want us to hold another election. Is that fair? Is that democracy? Are we going to let them change the course of history, so it stands in their favour and not ours? Should they hold the fate of our nation in the hands? Or should we hold it? Should we own it? For it is not in the stars to hold our destiny but in ourselves. Let us build the road from which our journey begins. They can have their re-election only when our lives have been improved. No more dehumanising plantation life. No more long hours of toil with small, small pay. Let us tell the foreigners that it was our great grandparents who established the great industries- rice, jewellery, timber. Industries which today keep this great nation afloat. It was our relatives who cleared, levelled and cultivated this vast land. This is our land! It will stay our land and we will be masters of our own destiny not the British or Dutch!"

Khan knew, as he stood in front of the ecstatic and ebullient crowd, that he had won the full support of the Indian community. How he wished he could do the same with the negroes.

Suddenly, the doors of the church burst open and British soldiers rushed into the sanctuary shouting and roughly corralling Khan's followers. Some Indians forcefully resisted being bludgeoned by the soldiers, but without warning a volley of bullets emptied into the crowd and several Indians fell onto the floor bloodied, injured and dead. Cries of murder echoed around the room, but the soldiers continued their merciless beatings and attacks on the unarmed crowd.

"Quick through this door!" urged one of Khan's aides.

Khan, Isabella, George and some of his entourage quickly exited the church and ran to the two vehicles which were parked at the back of the building. As they got in their vehicles, several British jeeps careered around the corner and tried to prevent the politician from escaping. However, as the British soldiers attempted a blocking manoeuvre on Khan's cars, a number of his bodyguards, who had remained outside the church, began firing back at their attackers giving their leader and his friends the window of opportunity to make good their escape.

"That was close," gasped Isabella trembling with fear and anger.

"I know!" replied her husband. "But I am not surprised."

"Why?"

"Because we have some spies in our organisation."

"How long have you known this and why haven't you told me? I thought we were watertight."

"No organisation is ever watertight, darling," Khan said kissing her on the cheek. "I have an idea, but it would be foolhardy of me to try and expose them without evidence."

"We need to find out who they are and quick," interjected George wiping a speck of blood from his lapel.

"You are right George. But believe me, we have to worry more about some of our so-called friends, our so-called allies, our so-called brothers before we can tackle the few quislings who are infecting our party."

"Who do you mean?" queried Isabella placing her husband's jacket, which she had picked up as they fled the church, on his knee.

"Well for a start," Khan's words trailed off as the car veered rapidly around a worker and his donkey in the middle of the road. "You can slow down now, Ali!" he continued as he straightened up on the back seat. "Who do I mean? Well one of our comrades who didn't attend the meeting today...."

"You mean Raymond Lloyd?" an astounded Isabella exclaimed. "Surely not."

Khan sat silently and looked at George. George knew that Khan was correct in his suspicions. George had witnessed Lloyd, De Witt and Sir Arthur Wilde meet on numerous occasions at the Wales Plantation. The cane-workers would often speak, deliberately in earshot of him, that nothing good would come from these meetings. Normally he would put these comments down to bias and prejudice but now he realised that a grain of truth lay in their suspicions.

"Why didn't he attend today? He is an ambitious man. And do you remember what Machiavelli said about ambition? *Men rise from one ambition to another, first they seek to secure themselves against attack and then they attack others*. Raymond is just that man."

"I don't believe it. He wouldn't compromise the party for individual glory?"

"You don't really know Raymond, Isabella," George said throwing a bloodied handkerchief out of the car window.

"I think George is right," Khan continued. "I have, from an excellent source, information that Raymond finds the idea of Indians exercising their right to build their own businesses anathema to his vision for British Guiana. Therefore, his continuing support of the G.P.P. must be brought into question together with the possibility of him achieving his ambition at all costs. And I mean at all costs."

9

"You'd better spend this wisely my friend."

Lloyd opened his wallet and counted out fifty US dollars, one by one, into Inty's hand.

"You've done a good job Inty. You deserve every cent, every dollar. We couldn't have done what we did without you. You'll do very well in my new party. Don't listen to Khan's nonsense that I am anti-Indian and pro-negro. I am pro- British Guiana and pro- Guianese. That means everyone, irrespective of their religion, colour or creed will share in the future prosperity of this wonderful country. That is if they follow me. Don't listen to him when he speaks of me as a man who only seeks power and fame. I am not a Macbeth, a Hitler ...a Stalin."

"Thank-you sir," Inty replied, shifting uncomfortably in the wooden chair he sat on in Lloyd's office in Church Street, Georgetown.

"If it wasn't for you Inty we would never have had found out what Subhan was doing. You certainly fooled George Winwick and his cronies."

Sweat trickled down Inty's temples and he felt pins and needles in his hands as he rested them on his knees. He looked at the burly negro bodyguards who stood imposingly behind Lloyd and a dark foreboding crossed his mind.

"Yes. You certainly are a chameleon of the highest order. You have to be otherwise you would never fool your enemy, would you?"

Inty remained silent and stared, like a rabbit caught in headlights, at his benefactor.

"I liken you Inty to Nathan Hale. Have you heard of him?"

Inty shrugged his shoulders.

"He was America's first spy. A man of inordinate principle and passion. He used disguises to hoodwink the British during the American War of Independence. Unfortunately, his luck ran out and he was captured and later executed. He was only twenty-one years of age. What a hero for the Americans," Lloyd paused and peered at Inty hoping for a reaction. "More importantly Inty. Nathan Hale was made famous not only for being a spy but also for his speech before his hanging in which he said *I only regret that I have but one life to lose for my country.* Do you know why I have retold this story to you?"

"No sir."

"I think you do Inty. I know you are more intelligent than you pretend to be. Why on earth do you think I agreed with my officers to select you to work for us?"

The dollar bills Inty held seemed to burn his hand with every word Lloyd uttered.

"Don't compare that money to thirty pieces of silver my friend. You deserve it and more. You, Nathan Hale and I would fight for our respective countries a thousand times in order that it would be liberated from the talons of the British Government."

Inty remained silent and scrunched the dollar bills so hard that his knuckles whitened.

"You know Inty," Lloyd continued nonchalantly. "We still need to discover the names of all the enemies of our state. The sooner we can find those worms who inveigle into our society and poison it, the better. Will you help us Inty? Will you be a disciple of the nation? Will you be a guardian for the Guianese state? Will you? Do you have any more names for us Inty? Do you?"

As he finished Lloyd pulled open a drawer and removed a large, brown envelope and handed it to Inty. Nervously he took it and looked inside.

"Two hundred dollars. All yours and more," smiled Lloyd. "As long as you provide us with some more information."

Inty looked at the money and then at the guards and finally at Lloyd.

"I have no more information Mr. Lloyd sir. Not at this time," he said fidgeting in his chair.

Lloyd remained silent. He stared deeply into Inty's eyes as if trying to hypnotize him in offering up more intelligence.

"All right Inty. I believe you," Lloyd lied. "Keep the money. Accept it as payment for any future information. I know I can rely on you. More importantly I know British Guiana can rely on you."

Inty rose from his chair, shook Lloyd's hand and slowly walked to the office door. As he turned the door handle and walked into the street Lloyd motioned to his bodyguards to follow him. Just before the two men exited the room, Lloyd stood up walked towards his employees and handed them a revolver each.

"You know what I need you to do," he said with a smirk on his face. "And bring back the cash. He won't need it where he's going to!"

10

Starbroek market, or the Big Market as it was known to the locals, was Dutch in ancestry and, originally, its buildings were of wooden construction and positioned on the land and water. It was here that, in 1792, slaves were allowed, for the first time, to sell plantains, on Sundays only, to supplement their meagre wages. Although over one hundred and fifty years had passed, the bazaars which inhabited the area cheek by jowl still provided most of its owners with a minimum living wage. The wooden edifices still existed but were fewer in number. Now shops were built from a mixture of concrete, zinc and iron. Here, British Guiana's underclass- Amerindians, Negroes, Chinese, Portuguese and Indians- the DNA of this vibrant, colourful trading community, coalesced to form a union of buyers and sellers.

George stood and circled three hundred and sixty degrees to experience the market's riot of colour, sounds and smells. As he soaked in the atmosphere, he reminisced on his former life in Liverpool when as a young boy he would, with his mother and father, walk to Stanley Market, situated on the dock road, on early Sunday mornings to buy goods and meet with friends to catch up on the weeks' news and gossip. The only difference really, he thought to himself, was the weather.

George meandered along the narrow passageways of Starbroek Market towards the Avenue of Republic. The fish and meat stalls were swarming, as usual, with people haggling over the price of salt- water fish like red snapper and fresh- water fish such as banga-mary or freshly slaughtered goats and groundhog meat. After a while he stopped at a stall to watch two Amerindian women, dressed in their traditional clothes, use a matapee to squeeze freshly grated cassava juice into metal bowls. The ingenuity of so-called illiterate people ceased to amaze him.

"Yuh wanna help mista," laughed the younger of the two women staring at him.

George tipped his Panama hat, smiled, and carried on walking. Stall after stall were piled high with bunches of callaloo, breadfruit, sapodilla, eddoes, guavas, okra, sugar cane and soursop. He was beginning to feel hungry and thirsty especially when he spied the Chinese spice stands and next to them, a number of snack stalls selling roti and curry, china cake, foofoo, metemgee, Portuguese garlic pork and Amerindian pepper pot.

"Mr. George."

George looked around for the voice calling his name.

"Over here, Mr. George!"

George located the voice. It was Inty. He was seated at one of the snack stalls eating a bowl of metemgee.

"Eat with me Mr. George. Yuh like eddoes, yam, cassava and plantain in coconut milk?"

"I certainly do, and I think I will, thank you Inty."

George sat next to his friend.

"Anuda metemgee, sista for Mr.George. And to drink?"

"I'll have a pawpaw milkshake please."

"Man," sighed Inty. "Yuh sure eat like a native."

"That's because of Beebi's influence," laughed George.

"That sista do yuh proud. Yuh lucky man. Many men wanted Beebi for der wife."

The Indian cook placed the bowl of metemgee and pawpaw milkshake in front of George. He took out a couple of dollar notes to pay when Inty quickly grabbed his hand.

"Nah. Mr. George. Yuh me guest. No pay."

George knew that it would be futile to argue with Inty because as with so many poor, impoverished men and women in British Guiana pride, honesty and the desire to give was always at the uppermost of their thoughts. To this end he admired and felt at ease with this community rather than the elite society his employment forced him to associate with.

"Thanks once again," George said taking a mouthful of metemgee.

"Are you shopping today Inty?"

"A little. Mr. George. But didn't yuh know about de meeting in Church street at two o'clock?" Inty whispered.

George took a sip of his cool, pawpaw drink.

"I did Inty," replied George. "But I sent my apologies. Work and Wilde's spies are complicating things for me at the moment, as you know."

"Me know, me know. I'm glad yuh back from yuh trip oversees. Ten months is a long time. Many bad things have happened since yuh bin away."

"I know. But we have to be careful. We don't want another Enmore. Do we?"

Inty finished his food, took a piece of roti and wiped the bowl clean.

"Yuh know Mr. George," Inty said, biting into a piece of roti. "Me no really care about dying. As long as me die for me country and countrymen. Der goin to be anuda Enmore. As sure as de coconut holds milk."

Inty took a swig from the Bank's beer bottle he was holding.

"Anuda ting Mr. George. Der too many workers starving. Dey av no dollar for eat with. Yuh wonda why cane-workers beat der missus and don't feed der pickaninnies? Dey ashamed man. Ashamed dat dey av no respect from de white man. Ashamed dat dey av to be whipped. Ashamed dat dey av der money taken if they sick. We av been sold into slavery agin Mr. George one hundred years after slavery bin don!"

George chewed on a slice of cassava and plantain. He knew that what Inty had said was true. Nothing on the plantations had really changed for the workers. Working practices of the nineteenth century still existed today both openly and behind closed doors. Indeed, he had heard from other plantation managers and overseers that Indians could still be jailed and fined for leaving the estate, refusing to start or finish work, insolence and vagrancy. Hans had informed him, with gay abandon, that he still sanctioned overseers setting tasks so hard that workers could not finish them on time. Unable to complete their work, the cane-cutters would be fined and Bookers, in turn, would save money as any worker who failed to finish his task got nothing at all. On the next day the worker had to start new again on another task.

Inty wiped his face with his hand, stood up and gave the Indian cook a fistful of coins.

"Yuh stay and enjoy yuh food Mr. George. Me let yuh know wah happen at meeting."

George watched as Inty disappeared into a sea of faces and bodies which seemed to be growing exponentially. He sat finishing his food and contemplated the life that Inty and his community had to endure. He knew, through the correspondence he had with his family back in Liverpool, that life for the poor in his hometown, especially after the war, was extremely gruelling and backbreaking but all things considered life in British Guiana, for the indigenous population, was like being back in the Dark Ages. He thought that maybe the stone age peoples of the world, the hunter-gatherers, had society mapped out more fairly than the so called modern age counterparts- at least the hunter gatherers realised the need for everyone to work together, in unison, for the good of the individual and their society as a whole. Moreover, he remembered that, at school, and even at such an early age, he disagreed with his classics teacher who put forward the Aristotelian theory that some men are slaves by nature. How he had argued, with his dumbfounded teacher listening impotently, could nature shape and form slaves, surely it was an artificial human construct to subjugate the poor? Indeed, he couldn't help but smile to himself when he remembered how he had cited Thomas Jefferson's seminal words *that all men are created equal*, to substantiate his point, when his teacher, exasperated, embarrassed and surprised that a fourteen- year old had dared question his teaching, expelled him from the classroom for insubordination. It was at this precise moment in time that he had decided to accept his Headmaster's request for him to sit the entrance exams for Oxford and Cambridge. He realised that he wanted to increase his knowledge and wanted to break free from the shackles of the cycle of poverty that he and innumerable boys and girls, of his class, had been fastened to due to an accidence of birth. He more than understood that gaining a degree from a first-class university would be a passport out of bondage and slavery. Moreover, he wanted, through reading History at university, to help change the world and the plight of the underclasses. Unfortunately, his academic aspirations had been cut short by the advent of World War Two.

"Yuh wan anuda pawpaw mista?" the stall owner enquired.

George smiled and shook his head. He got up and proceeded to walk in the direction of the Avenue of Republic passing jewellery and gold stalls, men fixing bicycles, furniture stands and livestock sellers. He enjoyed his weekly walks around Georgetown. It was me time. Time when he could gather his thoughts, ruminate about his life and consider the future. As he reached the Avenue of Republic, he stopped by the Law courts and studied the statue of Queen Victoria which had been erected in honour of her majesty as a testimony to British Imperialism. Memories of a similar statue, designed by F. M. Simpson and erected in James Street, Liverpool flooded into his mind as he recalled climbing to the top of her bronze crown with his friends on a Saturday afternoon after they had visited the penny matinees at the local Gaumont cinema.

His memory bubble was peremptorily burst when he felt a light tug on his white, linen trousers. George looked to his side and saw a small Amerindian boy, no more than four years old, holding out his dirty, grimy small, bony hand and smiling a toothless grin.

"Dollar, Master. Please!"

George looked at the boy's torn, filthy vest, shorts which

billowed around his scrawny legs and his blackened, calloused feet. Painfully thin with light brown skin and gaunt looks the boy, despite his obvious poverty, still possessed that sparkle of happiness and optimism that is roughly worn down, like the soles of old shoes, by life as a person grows old. George diverted his gaze to the surrounding crowd. On his arrival in British Guiana he had been warned about pickpockets, brigands, prostitutes and scheming adults who used young children as tools for their nefarious activities.

"Dollar, Master!"

George felt another tug on his trousers and noticed a brown thumbprint on his thigh. He pulled out a few paper dollars from his pocket and handed it to the boy who skipped away further into the market. He grinned and watched as the boy stopped by a watermelon seller and handed over one of the dollar notes in return for a large slice of juicy, red fruit. In an instant the boy gnawed into to the soft fruit and black seeds oozed from the corners of his mouth. Still chewing and with water etching a Picasso pattern onto his cheeks the boy turned to him, waved and disappeared into the crowd, watermelon in hand.

George turned and sauntered further along the Avenue of Republic. Nearby, he marvelled at the Parliament Building, designed by Joseph Hadfield, which was renowned as a symbol of hope and justice. It was here, he had learnt, that so many of British Guiana's emancipated slaves were able to purchase, for the very first time, their own land. A few moments later, he stopped and gazed at St. Andrew's Kirk, the oldest surviving structure of any church in British Guiana and an excellent example of Gothic architecture. As he studied the building he mused at its significance as a metaphor for the future of the country.

After a while he reached Church street and walked towards his favourite building, St. George's Cathedral - the world's tallest wooden constructed, free standing edifice. He loved everything about this structure especially its exterior Gothic façade with flying buttresses, central tower and the Latin cross formation of nave and transepts. Whenever he was in Georgetown, he would ensure that he spent some quality time inside the building in quiet contemplation.

George climbed up the several steps leading to the entrance of the cathedral and stepped in from the bright sunlight of the street to the dark, cool interior of the building. Directly opposite him, from the central aisle, was a magnificent altar with a chancel screen and electrolier and further along the corridor a banner of St. George and the Dragon hung next to one of many of the beautiful cathedral's stained- glass windows. Walking past an ornate, eagle brass lectern and sedilia, which was donated by the Chinese, he stopped in front of carved figures of Christ, Our Lady and St. John which lay behind the altar on the back wall. George bowed his head and crossed himself. After a minute in silent contemplation he looked up at the carved figures once again and noticed a shimmering iridescent light bouncing off Our Lady. The sunlight streaming through an adjacent stained - glass window had created the colourful effect, which culminated in the robes of Our Lady appearing a deep blue highlighted with gold and red. George was mesmerized.

"I thought I'd find you here."

George recognised the voice and turned, immediately, to see Beebi standing smiling in front of him wearing a figure- hugging red, polka dotted halter-necked dress with matching red gloves, red stilettos and red parasol. The light streaming through the windows created a halo effect around her head and a radiance shone from her face which made his heart skip a beat. She was to him beauty personified.

"My you do scrub up well," he said teasingly as held her tiny waist and lovingly kissed her soft lips.

Walking hand in hand out from the shade of the church into the bright light of the street he placed his Panama hat back onto his head and Beebi opened her parasol to protect herself from the rays of the hot sun. As they navigated the steps George tripped on the shoelace of one of his brown brogues. Stooping down to retie his laces he noticed that weeds were exerting their influence on the usually immaculate manicured lawn which encircled the cathedral.

"That's odd?" George said to Beebi. "It's unlike Subhan not to maintain the grounds."

"Yes. Since you got my brother the job he's usually been on time. I'll speak to Uncle Ramadeen who lives in Tiger Bay. Subhan's lodging with him now so he can be close to his work."

"Is he sick?"

George asked the question not out of curiosity but because of his genuine concern for the well- being of his brother-in-law. One of the reasons why the bishop of the cathedral and shop-owners in Church street agreed to employ Subhan was because of George's persuasive ability. But, since his return from studying abroad, he had heard, unlike Beebi, disturbing rumours that Subhan, for one reason or another, had started to neglect his work duties and had turned to alcohol.

"I don't think so George. I'll find out for you."

"Thanks darling," he pulled Beebi closer to him once more and kissed her cheek. "Listen I haven't told you enough, since my return, how much I missed you. I couldn't wait to get back to see you."

"But don't you miss your family back home? You said one day you'd like to go back to stay."

"Maybe one day, after I get the new management post. I could then transfer to an equivalent post back in England."

"You'll get it. They know how good you are. Who else could do the job?"

George was just about to reply when a chewing gum landed in front of him. To his side stood two thin black Africans who smiled with hatred at the couple.

"Hey yellow belly. Yuh like coolie wimin. Me like em too!" The smaller of the men said as he moved menacingly towards Beebi.

George pulled her to the opposite side of him and squared up to the taller of the two negroes. This had the desired effect as the bravado of both men evaporated when he, unseen by Beebi, opened his jacket to reveal to the men a holster with a Smith and Western model chambered twenty- five target revolver. The men stepped, slowly, back into a white, wicker fence and held their hands up in fear. Seconds seemed to be like hours for Beebi as she watched her husband standing like a lion ready to pounce on his prey. Suddenly, she grabbed his arm and with all her force pulled him away from the situation.

"Leave dem George. Dey nobody. Jus fools!"

George continued walking but turned to look at the two negroes as they laughed, back slapped each other and cursed him. Blood started to pump through his veins and his anger began to rise. Beebi could feel the tension and carried on pulling him forward.

"Don't yuh mind dem! We go an hav good time!" Beebi shouted, loudly, so the men could hear her.

With Beebi leading him quickly from the confrontation George's anger started to subside like a tsunami ebbing back to its point of origin but he realised that he had upset his young wife as whenever she resorted to speak pidgin English he knew that trouble was just around the corner

"Man, I dunno why can't yuh jus ignore dose fools."

Beebi and George proceeded to walk in the direction of the botanical gardens without speaking to one another. Eventually George took hold of his wife's hand and apologised.

"That's okay George. But, no reason for you to lose your life over chewing gum. Is there?"

"Your right, your always right."

Beebi started to cry. She pulled out a silk, white handkerchief from her handbag and dabbed her eyes.

"Hey, hey. No need for tears. All's well that ends well. Don't cry. I wouldn't risk my life needlessly. I would have walked away!"

"Would you?"

"Of course! I would never put you or Steven in danger. Never!"

They carried on walking in the hot sun holding hands admiring the artificial lakes bordering the gardens.

"By the way did you do much while I was away?"

Beebi stopped on a bridge arching over one of the lakes. She said nothing. She stared into the waters below and watched the ripples get larger and larger as dark clouds blew across through the air partially blocking out the sun.

"Penny for your thoughts!"

Beebi remained pensive and quiet.

"If you don't want to talk, you don't have to darling."

"Look over there. Look!" Beebi, without facing her husband, pointed to a head of an animal swimming in the distance. "What is it?"

George stared at the creature as it neared the bridge and clambered onto a rocky promontory situated near to a grassy bank.

"It's a manatee." George replied.

The couple, leaning on the bridge, stared at the large, grey mammal as it dived in and out of the water every minute or so. This was the first time he had witnessed the ponderous creatures behave so erratically. Indeed, he had noted that they usually rested under water for over twenty minutes and when swimming surfaced for oxygen at a few minutes a time. Suddenly, the manatee dived under the water again only to resurface directly below Beebi. The creature's wrinkled, whiskered snout seemed to be inhaling her scent. It seemed to be mysteriously, almost intuitively, connecting with her psyche. Beebi felt faint. As she stared into the manatee's black eyes, she felt a foreboding, her knees buckled, and she sank to the floor dropping her parasol.

"Beebi! What's the matter are you okay?" George said helping her to her feet. "You fainted! Is it the heat? Have you eaten today?"

Beebi rested her head on his chest and through a hazy gaze saw the manatee submerge once again.

"I'm fine, I'm fine," she said wiping her forehead with her white handkerchief. "It must be the heat."

Beebi slid from George's gentle embrace and as she did so she noticed the manatee again. However, maybe due to her dizzy spell she thought that the manatee looked somewhat different.

What seemed familiar, however, was the intense connectedness between it and herself. She watched as the manatee clambered, ignominiously, onto some rocks adjacent to the bridge.

"That must be its partner," said George as he peered over the bridge pointing to another smaller manatee swimming towards the rocks. "It looks as if the first manatee is pregnant."

Beebi swooned and fell into George's arms.

"Come on. I am taking you home," George said.

Suddenly, from out of nowhere, several bullets could be heard popping, like firecrackers, in the distance. George instinctively pulled Beebi to the ground and sheltered her with his massive body.

"Keep down, love! Keep down!" George peered from underneath his arms and could see people dashing for cover. "It's coming from those houses over there."

His five years in the British Army had implanted into his long- term memory a bank of firearm information which now had proved to be of immense value. Although only small arm fire, he realised that he and Beebi were within easy range of the gun and could be inadvertently killed. He lay motionless, Beebi underneath him, for about a minute. Silence ensued. Just as he was about to rise, he heard the roar of heavy vehicles and the deafening sound of sub-machine gun fire, followed by the staccato volley of handguns. He buried his head deep within Beebi's lower back whilst pressing her head firmly on the floor as bullets careered round them and ricocheted off the iron bridge stripping off the white paint. Beebi whimpered in pain and fear.

"Stay still darling, don't move! Please don't move!"

Shouts, screams, gunfire and engines fused together no more than one hundred feet from where the couple cowered. Time stood still. Numerous thoughts raced through his mind. Get up and run for safer cover! Jump over the bridge into the water? Crawl back to the brow of the bridge? Where they going to be shot? Who was shooting at whom and why? Stay put and wait?

"It's okay man! Yuh can get up."

George moved his hand to his gun and looked at the negro who was standing over him and Beebi.

"Dey got der man."

The negro smiled and pointed to houses on Church street. George stood up and helped Beebi to her feet. He turned, looked and saw a squad of Welsh Fusiliers, guns in hand, jumping out of jeeps and lorries and forming a guard around the area of disturbance.

"That was close. We'd better get back home. It's not safe at the moment," he said as he held Beebi tightly against his body.

Dazed and upset Beebi extricated herself from George and walked, unsteadily, a few paces to the to the bridge and looked out into the lake. Suddenly, she let out an unholy scream and fainted, George rushed to her side and peered through the bridge's metal rails. There on the rock lay the first manatee dead, shot in the stomach by the indiscriminate gunfire, exposing a bloodied foetus.

11

George looked at the dishevelled body which lay sprawled along a bench in a small, wooden rum shop in downtown Georgetown. Wearing a filthy, ripped shirt, trousers baggy and torn and sole- less shoes tied with string the drunk resembled a scarecrow who had been attacked by a group of savage dogs. George brushed the drunk's unshaven face with his hand.

"How many has he had?" he asked the innkeeper.

"Too many, Mister," the innkeeper said indifferently, whilst cleaning a glass. "He no good! I about to throw him out. He no pay for a week now."

George took out his wallet, gave the innkeeper a handful of dollars, moved the drunk's legs and sat down next to him.

"Why yuh here Mr. George?" the drunk slurred. "He make a big thing about me drinkin' but is he who give it me. He know me good for de money."

"Subhan! Listen! Beebi sent me to bring you home."

"Beebi! Beebi!" Subhan raised his thin body and exposed a toothless sarcastic grin. "Beebi? She is my keeper? Me young sister is now me mama? Is that right Mr. George? She tell me what to do? I me own man Mr. George." Subhan bent down and lifted an empty bottle of Banks's beer and put it to his mouth.

"I'm here to help Subhan!" George replied taking the bottle from him. "We're all concerned. I'm trying to get you another job in the fields."

"Me na wanna work in de fields Mr. George. The sun will kill me man. Get me job like before Mr. George. Den I come."

George looked deeply into Subhan's bloodshot eyes. He had

helped his brother-in-law on several occasions, but his help had been thrown back into his face as Subhan, due to his predilection for self-destruction, alcoholism and depression, continually failed to stick to the employment that George had secured for him. How could he promise Subhan another caretaking job?

"I'll see what I can do for you," George lied. "Let's get out of here and get some food for you."

George lifted Subhan and dragged him out of the rum shop, across a bridge and down Regent Street. Off duty British, American and Canadian servicemen meandered in between the brightly lit buildings which doubled up as brothels and cafes and Negro street girls paraded themselves hoping to secure an illicit assignation.

"Hey mista yuh like?"

A skinny, young negro girl, no more than twelve years old, leaned against a shop door. George noticed her slender waist, soft dark brown skin and pubescent nipples protruding from an old, pink tight, fitting camisole.

"Yuh an yuh friend come with me," the girl said flirtatiously.

"We go inside Mr. George. Me buy her for yuh!"

Subhan tried to steer George into the girl's direction but George lifted him as if he were a sack of coal and carried him on his shoulder down the street. George could hear the giggles of the girl disappearing into the distance as he reached one of Georgetown's many cook shops.

"Hello Mr. George. Yuh bring rubbish to me shop?"

"He's my brother –in-law Haliman."

"Me know who he is," Haliman cursed as she saw George lay Subhan on a chair.

Haliman walked over to George and placed a kerosene lamp on the table and lit it. As she walked back to her cooking pot, she deliberately hit Subhan on the head with a metal ladle. Subhan let out a low moan and got up to follow the cook but George, mindful of Subhan's drunken state, held onto him securely and as he did so he noticed the outline of a large middle- aged Indian man sitting down to a plate of roti and curry opposite them.

As the Indian man ate his supper, Haliman brought two bowls of shrimp and callaloo soup and placed them in front of George and Subhan. George watched as Haliman returned to her cooking stove ripped several pieces of pre-prepared flour dough, rolled one out and placed it on a flat heavy metal plate which sizzled with the oil she had just drizzled on top. He watched fascinated as Haliman moved the dough against the plate with her bare hands. How on earth she didn't burn herself never ceased to amaze him even after all the years he had frequented her cook house. In no more than a few minutes the first of several rotis were made. When Subhan saw Haliman walk towards them with the freshly cooked breads he attempted to snatch one out of the old lady's hand but Haliman, mindful of the antics of drunks such as Subhan, quickly sidestepped his outstretched arm, placed them in front of George and turning to walk back to her stove deliberately cuffed Subhan on the back of his neck causing him to spill a mouthful of shrimps back into his bowl.

"Fool!" Haliman snarled to herself.

"Wah yuh do dat for?" moaned Subhan picking up a hot roti.

"Don't upset her anymore," whispered George. "Otherwise you might get another smack,"

"She crazy old woman," slurred the drunk dipping his roti into the soup and devouring it regardless of the mess he made. "Me not know why yuh bring me here Mr. George. Me prefer Regent Street food!"

The Indian man finished his meal, thanked Haliman and stood up. George had seen many tall, well-built Indian men, usually of Sikh origin, in British Guiana but had not seen many who looked as if they originated from South India or Ceylon. As the Indian man walked out of the cook house, he stole a look at George, but fixed his gaze on Subhan. George wondered why the man held such an interest in Subhan. Maybe he was disgusted at the sight of a drunk sitting with a white man. Maybe he knew Subhan – but if he did why not acknowledge him? Maybe he was a plain clothed policeman who wanted to remember Subhan for future reference. In any case George felt ill at ease but his thoughts were quickly interrupted at the sound of Subhan retching into his bowl.

"Man get this fool out of me cookhouse!" cussed Haliman looking at Subhan sprawled face first on the table, soup covering his already soiled trousers and shrimps resting on his cheeks. "Yuh understand wah me say?"

George looked at Haliman who held a large kitchen knife and pointed it menacingly at the drunk.

"Haliman!" cajoled George mopping the soup with some rag towels and looking imploringly at the old lady. "Help me out here. Please. I need to help Subhan."

Haliman didn't move or say anything for a moment or two. She liked and respected George. Of all the white men she had met in her seventy-five years he was the most decent, kind and friendly. He had, she thought, a moral compass which continually faced the right direction. A god-fearing woman herself, who went to church every Sunday even though she was a Muslim, Haliman's bark was worse than her bite. She had lived on the planet for too many years to be upset by drunks, vagabonds and profligates. Indeed, one of the reasons why her business did well was not because of her culinary expertise but because, despite her hard exterior, she would always give food or time to whoever needed it.

"Me nah know!" Mr. George. "Me nah know why yuh bother with dis man. He no good."

"He's my brother-in-law Haliman! As you well know. I've got to help him."

Haliman put down her knife and collected some old rags from the side of her stove. She had always liked Subhan, despite his fall from grace. She remembered him being the apple of his mother's eye not because of his dark, handsome features or his boyish sense of humour but because he was kind, generous and clever. Indeed, he was academically gifted, an excellent cricketer and the person, most people believed, who would escape the confines of poverty by going to university and embarking upon a career in politics. Unfortunately for him, Haliman mused, Fate had knocked on his door and dealt him in adolescence and his twenties an unhappy hand of life-cards which had led to his present state. Despite her outward belligerent behaviour towards Subhan she had a soft spot for him and always ensured he had a hot meal everyday regardless if he could pay or not.

"Well yuh do wah yuh ave to do Mr. George. Me no time for de pickaninny."

Haliman retired to the back of her cookhouse and began washing the cutlery in a plastic bowl. Between the clanking of knives and forks and the swishing of water George could hear Haliman cursing the world and its mother.

"Are you feeling any better?" George shook Subhan's bony arm. "Can you stand up?"

"Leave me be Mr. George. Leave me be! Me wanna sleep. Sleep in peace."

"No, no, you don't. Drink this!" George held a tin cup of coffee and began feeding it down Subhan's throat.

After a few moments Subhan wiped his mouth, screwed his eyes and stared Intently at George.

"Wah yuh want Mr. George? Wah yuh want?"

"I need you to tell me the truth Subhan. The truth! Do you know who killed Inty? Who told the authorities about the meeting?"

On hearing these words Subhan sat up straight as a bolt as if he had just been electrocuted. He diverted his gaze from George and looked all around himself fearing that he was being watched.

"You must tell me the truth! You, me, Beebi, the party are all in danger. I can't help unless I know everything Subhan. Think, Think! The truth!"

"Mr. George. Me nah know anything. Anything!" He replied sweating profusely.

George took up a harder stance. His voice became deeper and he rolled his words with surety. His blue eyes pierced the veil of lies emanating from Subhan's dark brown gaze.

"I am not going to waste my time with you Subhan. Time is of the essence. I need to know the truth now. Not tomorrow or next week. Now! Forget your own miserable existence. Think of your sisters... think about the future of British Guiana!"

Subhan cleared his throat, "I nah know anything Mr. George. Upon me life. Me tell truth!"

"Your life might be cut short. Don't you know what you have done? Tell me. Who was your contact? Tell me!"

George grabbed Subhan by the arm and although Subhan tried to resist, George's iron grip immobilized him so that all he could do was wince with pain.

"Please, please, Mr. George let go me!"

"Tell me, tell me," George menacingly murmured as he added more purchase to his grip. "You don't know what you have done but we can sort things out as long as you give me all the information!"

"Mr. George, okay, I tell you."

As George released his grip Subhan leapt to his feet, pushed the wooden table against his brother-in-law and darted into the dark night leaving George sprawled on the floor. Quickly, George got to his feet and ran after the fleet footed drunk across the street into the shadowy neighbourhood where very few lights shone. After several minutes of searching he reached the bridge which an hour or so before he had frogmarched Subhan. He stopped, took a deep breath and scanned the dimness for his prey. What a fool had he been he thought to himself. Why on earth did he let go of him? At the back of his mind he knew that Subhan would try to escape. He had done so many times before... from criminals, debtors and police. On many such occasions George had to go and persuade him to surrender himself to the police or pay off his debtors and convince them not to lend him anymore monies. Now it was too late! Subhan had melted into the darkness of the Guianese night and with him the chance to discover who had murdered Inty and more importantly who was behind the infiltration of the G.P.P.

12

Subhan's emaciated, canal- soaked body lay on four greenheart planks on the floor of Beebi's house in Meten -Meer -Zorg, West Coast Demerara. A negro policeman stood next to the body like Cerberus guarding the gates to the daunting underworld. George and Khartoon engaged the policeman in small talk until Beebi arrived running and out of breath. Her dress clung to her body tightly, as the heat of the day mixed with her own perspiration, conspired to sodden her clothes. On seeing her brother laying wet and lifeless on the floor, she wailed like a banshee. Tears streamed from her eyes and she fell onto her knees and cradled Subhan's limp head in her lap.

"My brother, my brother! Allah! Why Allah! Why! My poor brother!"

Khartoon placed her arm around her sister's shoulders to comfort her whilst George stood gazing at Subhan's corpse.

"Let it out sista, let it out! He gone to a better place dan dis. He free now! He no pain. He in Paradise!"

Beebi let out another throat curdling wail and buried her head into the thin chest of her brother. Khartoon looked at George and beckoned him towards her sister. George walked slowly over to his wife and touched her shoulder. Beebi looked imploringly at him, grabbed his hand and held it tightly

Khartoon strode over to a drinks' cabinet and poured out a glass of rum. After taking a sip of the alcohol herself, she handed the glass to Beebi who reluctantly drank it in one shot.

"How did it happen?" Beebi quizzed the policeman.

The constable shrugged his shoulders. "Sista, me don't know.

Someone spot de body in canal dis morning, in town, near Regent Street. Me think he was drunk, and he just fall in. But me do know that if yuh don't get him buried soon he'll stink the place!"

Khartoon kissed her teeth and snarled, "If yuh finish yuh business leave dis house. Yuh no respect for de dead man?"

The constable, unconcerned, turned, place his cap back on his head and walked slowly out of the house and down the path shaking his head.

George squeezed Beebi's hand in support, but guilt began to flood over him. Had he been the cause of Subhan's death? Did his actions at the cook shop result in him falling into the canal? Even worse did Subhan kill himself? George's mind churned those thoughts over and over until Khartoon's voice brought him back into the present.

"Mr. George, will yuh organise things? Me have to look after BeebI. The doctor will come soon."

"Of course, Khartoon," George replied lifting Beebi up and leading her to the bedroom. "I'll arrange everything via my office. Don't you worry."

13

The following day crowds of over two hundred mourners sat huddled in the local Masjid's courtyard just around the corner from Beebi's house in anticipation of Subhan's funeral. Although the third largest religious group in British Guiana, Muslims were frequently denied constructing formal Masjid's or Mosques on plantations. Indeed, ever since the eighteenth century, colonialists had been successful, by hook or by crook, in forcing their West African Fula Muslim slaves to abandon their faith so that by the middle of the nineteenth century the Fula's had completely lost their religious identity. However, the colonialists attempt to replicate their anti-Muslim plan with the indentured Indians, who were brought to British Guiana after 1838 when Guiana had become a colony of the England, proved less effective and successful. As such, although not having the finances to build Masjid's, many Indian Muslims would mark off an area, in a traditional Islamic manner, to signify a sacred place where Muslim's would meet in the open to initiate ritual worship. However, In Meten-Meer-Zorg, the indentured Indians had in fact progressed from merely marking off an area to that of constructing their first Masjid made of mud and palm leaves much to the annoyance of Bookers and especially Hans and Mr. De Witt.

George stood outside Beebi's house and peered through the window as Subhan's brothers conducted the Islamic Ghusi and Kafan rituals on his deceased brother-in law. He watched as they gently, carefully and respectfully washed and massaged sweet smelling frankincense into every pore of Subhan's emaciated and discoloured body in an orderly, planned manner head to feet. Then, he looked forlornly, as the men covered the body with three white sheets, tied a rope around the legs, a rope around the head and two ropes around the midriff so that they could lift the small shroud and carry it out into the bright afternoon daylight.

Beebi and Khartoon cried piteously as they saw their deceased brother being ferried out of the house by their siblings and tearfully followed the body as it was transported to the Masjid for funeral prayers. When the funeral cortege eventually arrived at the Masjid, George noticed that many guests had arranged themselves into three formal rows, facing Mecca, with the closest male members of the family standing in the first row. Behind the other male mourners, children and women were assembled and recited verses from the Koran until the body of Subhan was brought to the front of the congregation and placed on large wooden table draped in a black cloth.

When George situated himself in the first row, he glanced towards the courtyard gates and noticed four army jeeps, brimming with Welsh Fusiliers armed with rifles, parked on either side of the driveway. As he squinted in the midday sun, he recognised the small be-spectacled figure of Mr. De Witt sitting on the back seat of one of the jeeps engaging in a jovial conversation with the unmistakeable elephantine figure of Hans, who was disrespectfully dressed in shorts and drank from a bottle of Bank's beer, together with the large Indian man he had seen in Haliman's cook shop. Why had De Witt decided to attend the funeral he thought? And why had he attended with soldiers? Surely, he couldn't be so foolish as to attempt to disrupt the funeral? Or had he heard of a potential uprising amongst the caneworkers because of Subhan's unexplained death?

After the mourners had finished reciting their verses and the Imam had completed his homily and reading from the Quran the congregation, in rows, passed Subhan's body from shoulder to shoulder towards the cemetery which lay directly opposite the Masjid. As the friends and relatives walked silently through the courtyard gates, laughter from Hans and De Witt could be heard and several mourners cast disapproving looks towards the two white men. George glared at Hans. Hans in turn took a long swig from the bottle he was holding and threw it casually against the Masjid's wall smashing it into myriads of pieces. A small, thin Indian man walking alongside George turned and was about to lunge at Hans when George grabbed him by the arm and quietly persuaded him not to rise to the bait.

At the cemetery, Subhan's body was placed on his right side into the grave, facing Mecca, whilst friends and relatives recited prayers and chanted *Bismalla wa ala millati rasulillah*. As with Islamic burial traditions, wood and stones were placed on top of the body so the soil did not come into direct contact with the deceased and afterwards the mourners each threw three handfuls of soil into the grave as a mark of respect and love. Finally, once the grave had been filled, the Imam placed a stone marker over it but as he did so a loud rumbling from the heavens suddenly interrupted the service. Thunderclaps could be heard nearby, and small raindrops began to pepper the mourners and the graveside. After several minutes, the heavens opened and, a deluge of rain cascaded onto the congregation below washing the final stone away into the nearby water drain exposing Subhan's corpse.

Despite the torrential rain George, Beebi, Khartoon and their close family and friends remained at the burial site whilst scores of mourners ran to the Masjid seeking sanctuary from the tropical downpour. Suddenly, a cacophony of tortured voices, a volley of gunfire and the heavy revving of jeep engines forced George to turn around and witness the brutal bludgeoning of numerous Muslims by groups of Welsh Fusiliers who had alighted from their vehicles whilst the funeral was in progress. He looked on impotently, as he saw several bloodied and severely injured male mourners being forcefully corralled and frogmarched into the back of the waiting jeeps. De Witt, George mused, had deliberately planned the provocative course of action knowing full well that suspected enemies of the state would, despite the likelihood of being discovered, attend Subhan's funeral. George trembled with rage and frustration at De Witt's opportunistic, insensitive and callous plan and vowed revenge. Disgusted, disheartened and deflated he diverted his gaze from the scene of carnage down below and noticed Beebi sprawled on top of her brother's final resting place crying inconsolably.

14

"Sorry to hear about your brother-in-law," Debbie said inhaling from her cigarette. "I know that you got him the job in Church Street and I believe he was doing really well at the start. I'm so surprised that he was double agent. He didn't seem the type. I mean he was so young. What a waste!"

Debbie began to cry, and tears rolled down her cheek leaving behind a rivulet of mascara. George thought about holding and comforting her but something from the past, the dim murky past of his childhood clouded his instinct to be emotionally literate, so he just stood and stared at his tearful friend.

"Is Beebi all right George? Is there anything I can do? Anything?"

Debbie threw her cigarette onto the floor and George watched as it continued to burn against the golden, yellow sand.

Suddenly he felt Debbie's arms tighten around his shoulders. He felt her nipples against his chest and her supple thighs resting close to his groin. The lemony aroma of her hair together with the subtle scent of her perfume overpowered his senses to such an extent that he felt weak at the knees. He closed his eyes and began to think of work issues rather than that of a beautiful woman holding him tightly in a state of sorrow. Slowly a life-force that he was desperately trying to suppress at the base of his abdomen began to awaken. He tried even harder to set the beast back to its slumber, but to no avail.

"Oh, I'm so sorry George. You must think me a fool! Sorry to be so emotional."

George's predicament was abruptly solved, and the beast returned to its rest as Debbie removed her embrace and stood looking, sadly, at him

"Don't be silly. It's only human to react as you did." George said smoothing his brylcreamed hair back.

"Yes. But George why did they kill him ...there were bigger fish they could have killed. Not a poor, defenceless man."

Debbie took out a small, clean, silk handkerchief from her purse and dabbed her eyes. George placed his left hand under her right elbow and guided her to the shade of a tree where at its base lay a tartan chequered rug, a picnic hamper, two glasses and a bottle of burgundy. As they both sat down a gust of wind blew sand across the rug and into the clean glasses. George quickly emptied the sand particles, opened the wine and poured it into the receptacles.

"Here! Take a sip of this. This will calm you down."

Debbie took the glass and drank slowly pondering on the death of Subhan.

"These things happen," George said as he opened the hamper and took out some fruit. "He was in the wrong place at the wrong time. But I agree I don't understand why they selected to eliminate him rather than a more important member."

"Maybe he was a pawn to be removed," Debbie replied placing the glass onto the rug. "An example to everyone else. Maybe they deliberately chose him because if they murdered one person it would be an example to everyone else of what they would do to potential spies."

George mused on the idea but realised that despite being a close friend he could not confide in her political matters let alone matters of the heart.

"That could be true. But we live in a politically unstable time. Look at what's happening around the globe in the other commonwealth countries! I'm sure the G.P.P. and British Government are not naïve enough to consider that they may not be infiltrated by spies- male or female!"

George glared, humorously, at Debbie.

"Don't you dare accuse me of being a spy," laughed Debbie as she threw a banana at George.

"For all I know you could be the new Mata Hari," teased George.

"And you Quisling."

"And you Josephine Baker."

"And you Robert Baden-Powell."

"Ok," George laughed. "You win."

They sat staring at each other for what seemed an eternity. Debbie's opalescent, brown eyes connected with George's deep blue eyes creating an instant hypnotic trance which the sounds of the lapping ocean waves, the sonorous birdsong of the Kiskadees' and the incessant rumble of trucks and cars from the nearby coast road could not break. Both knew that they liked, if not loved, each other but realised that breaking their marriage vows, as committed Catholics, would be anathema not only to their spouses and family but also to the Pope and what he represented. Catholicism was ingrained into every pore of their being and despite temptation and the thought of personal gratification both knew they could not break God's Law.

"This is good chicken, Winwick!"

Debbie and George's connected bubble burst as they recognized Han's voice. He stood above them wearing black shorts which were too tight for his muscular, blonde hairy thighs and a yellow-orange Hawaiian short-sleeved shirt which blended into his sunburnt skin. He held onto the tiny waist of a pretty, skinny, negro girl, no more than thirteen years of age, who appeared embarrassed and uncomfortable in the company of the huge German.

"Do you like?" laughed Hans pointing to the girl. "Her name is Papillon. Butterfly to you George. Pretty name for a pretty girl eh?" Hans proceeded to violently kiss the youngster and maul her left breast with his massive white hand. Debbie looked away in disgust.

"Schmeckt. Tastes like your wife, Englishman."

George began to stand but Debbie grabbed his arm tightly and shook her head.

"I wonder if Mr. De Witt knows about your secret rendezvous with your lover."

At this George shrugged Debbie's hand away, stood and squared up to Hans. The young girl cowered behind her sugar-daddy and Debbie, quick as lightning, stepped in between the two men.

"Du Sau. Ich werde meinem Mann von Ihren Anspielungen erzähle. How dare you. He will know what you have intimated!"

"Yah! Yah! What do the filthy English say kein rauch ohne feuer! No smoke without fire! Ha! Ha! Kommen meine kleine hure! Let's leave them to their secret whispers." Hans threw the chicken bone onto the picnic rug, pulled the young negro girl to him squeezing her small, bony backside and led her in the direction of the coastal road.

"What a pig of a man. I don't know what my husband sees in him. He's morally bankrupt!" shouted Debbie angrily.

"He's good at his job and he's good at bullying people. You should have let me hit him."

"And what good would that have done?"

"Well satisfied my ego for a start."

"Then you would be no better than him. I thought you were different George!"

"He needs to be taught a lesson. Sooner rather than later."

"I don't think he can learn anything. He's too set in his ways. I've never liked him. How long has he been in British Guiana?"

"Less than six years. He arrived just before you. Your husband headhunted him from Holland."

"Sometimes even my husband can make mistakes."

George and Debbie laughed and watched Hans disappear into the distance.

"Bookers would be in a far less strong position without your husband's management skills."

Debbie paused for a moment before answering. "You are right George but sometimes morality comes before profit. I'd sooner they have smaller profits and be able to sleep at nights and employ decent human beings rather than mean, menacing self-serving individuals like Hans."

George took a sip of wine and smiled at Debbie.

"I agree with you, but to the likes of your husband and Hans there's no sentiment in making money. That's why your husband employed Hans. He knows that he can get results by hook or by crook. He knows who he wants, why he wants them and when to get rid of them."

"Are you saying my husband is heartless, callous and emotionless?" teased Debbie brushing her hair in place as a cool breeze wafted over them.

"Of course not," an embarrassed George replied. "I'm sure you wouldn't have married such a person."

"Are you sure?" Debbie said mischievously. "I might have married for love or I might have married for convenience. What do you think?"

George blushed deeply and thought for a moment. What should he say? The truth? No! That may upset her, and it would be the last thing he would want to do? A lie? No! Debbie would see through that also and equally be offended. He was stymied by the question. As he contemplated the question, he remembered Napoleon Bonaparte's famous quote *Nothing is more difficult, and therefore more precious, than to be able to decide.* Why couldn't he make a decision under these circumstances? How could it be that in matters of the heart he was indecisive, hesitant and incapable of instantaneous judgements but in matters of work and business he was resolute, unyielding and active?

"I'm sorry George," interjected Debbie conscious of embarrassing him. "That was wicked of me. You don't have to answer that question. I was just teasing you. Of course, I married...for love. Which girl, in their right mind wouldn't?"

Suddenly, the breeze grew stronger and drove particles of sand into Debbie's eye causing her to wince and blink.

"Hold still," said George, and to his own amazement, he pulled out his unused handkerchief, wetted it with spittle and extracted the grains of sand lodged in the corner of her right eye. As he was removing the sand. he could feel the sweet breath of Debbie caressing his neck and the soft, velvet grip of her left hand on his right hand. His hands trembled as she touched his skin and electrical impulses spiralled, once again, towards his lower abdomen. Seconds seemed like minutes as the two friends held each other in a compromising position.

"Mr. George!"

George's attention flew to where the voice was emanating from but as he turned to look at the person addressing him, he inadvertently jabbed Debbie's eye with his covered index finger.

"Christ I'm sorry!"

"Never mind," Debbie said softly taking his handkerchief and removing the rest of the sand particles.

"Is Mrs. De Witt okay. Mr. George? Sorry to interrupt but I have something important to tell you as a matter of urgency."

George stood up and realized that the well- dressed figure standing before him was none other than Ali Persaud.

15

Bourda, or Georgetown Cricket Club, as it was fondly known, was first established in 1884. It owned one of the oldest cricket grounds in the Caribbean used by the Guianese cricket team to host local and international test matches. Located between Regent street and North Road the ground was famous for its unprotected moat and its cantilever stands.

"He's a good batsman," Wilde remarked to De Witt.

The managers dressed in white blazers and black linen trousers watched as George struck the oncoming cricket ball with such force that it was sent skywards into the opposite cantilever stand for six magnificent runs.

"Pity he won't be here for long," snarled Hans jealously.

The crowd cheered vociferously as George raised his bat in acknowledgement of the half century he had just made. The annual Booker Plantation cricket final was one of the most prestigious events on the ex-patriate social calendar. It was also the one event that the Indian and Negro plantation workers were allowed to attend in order that a carnival atmosphere could reverberate around the ground.

"Who wants to wager that George will make his century?" De Witt said opening his black leather wallet and placing five crisp one-hundred dollars on the table in front of him.

Wilde, Lloyd and Hans all offered a counter bet to De Witt's wager and watched in earnest as George elegantly drove the next ball mid-wicket for four runs. Whistles of delight and clinking of bottles echoed from the moat where a contingent of Wales plantation workers stood and sat on seeing the ball jump over the rope skirting the cricket pitch.

'Double or quit?" De Witt said as one of the Negro servants gave him a gin cocktail.

"Too rich for me," Wilde replied. "He's in the zone. I'll stick to the five hundred."

"I'll take up you offer," said Hans placing a further five hundred dollars on the table. "I don't have any confidence in the Englishman at all. Just wait till the spinner comes on. The fool will be bamboozled and lose his wicket."

The men sipped their drinks and watched as a fast bowler ran in at a thunderous pace and hurled the ball onto the middle of the wicket, with such brute force, that it bounced ferociously upwards and struck George heavily and squarely on the chest.

"My God, what a ball!" shouted Wilde as he watched George stand unflinching as the ball bounced into the hands of the silly mid- off. "He must be made of steel. How on earth can he still be standing up after being hit so hard?"

The men watched as the players and umpires encircled George out of a deep concern that he was seriously injured. After several minutes they walked back to their positions and the crowd clapped in appreciation as George gestured that he was ready to continue.

"That's typical of the man...stubborn to the point of self-destruction," De Witt said admiringly.

"More to the point of stupidity," replied Hans quietly and sarcastically finishing his drink.

"Now Hans. You have to learn to give credit where credit is due! Not many men would continue batting let alone not collapse to the floor after being bludgeoned so brutally."

Hans stood up angrily and marched to the bathroom. As he did so he glanced in the direction of George who guided the ball once again deftly off his legs to the boundary for four more runs.

"I think Hans hatred for George borders on the pathological," mused Wilde taking off his boater.

"That maybe a blessing in disguise," replied De Witt with a twinkle in his eye. "Considering our concerns over George's recent activities."

"He certainly hasn't listened to his uncle and he certainly hasn't taken any notice of the memos that have been distributed to your European staff," Lloyd added biting into a cucumber sandwich. "I like the man. He has principles. But sometimes you have to see the bigger picture and I don't think he does."

"I agree," interjected Wilde. "If the British are to continue to rule this land and bring peace and prosperity, any thoughts of insurgence and talk of independence must be squashed with an iron fist. We can't risk dealing with the matter in a democratic manner. That's why we've asked you to join us in usurping the G.P.P."

"I understand your viewpoint," Lloyd replied. "You know that historically Khan and I sought to work together for the betterment of British Guiana. Unfortunately, strategic differences have led us to part company, but I still think we can agree on matters of policy if we are given time to do so."

"As the Japanese say *time waits for no one*. We can't afford to wait...look what happened in India," Wilde retorted. "If we had nipped the insurrection in the bud there wouldn't have been any independence."

Suddenly a loud roar came from the field of play. The men looked and saw George raising his bat in acknowledgement after scoring another six runs.

Hans returned, pulled his chair back and slumped into it with a black frown spread across his face.

"You haven't lost your bet yet Hans. Don't worry," smiled De Witt. "Have another beer."

"Never mind George's innings I hear that you have eliminated an enemy of ours who was causing us a lot of grief," Wilde said looking at Hans in admiration. "Good work my German friend. I don't know what you did to him, and I don't want to know. But you certainly extricated a lot of secret information which will benefit us in usurping the G.P.P."

"Subhan was a lazy coolie drunk," snarled Hans, "It was easy getting names from him ...like stealing sweets from a baby."

"Well it confirmed our suspicions that George is playing a pivotal role in disseminating confidential information to Khan. We have to organize a surveillance unit to discover who his accomplices are," continued Wilde. "And I...I mean we think you would be the ideal person to head the group. What do you think?"

Hans stared earnestly and solemnly into the eyes of each of the men in the room and an evil smile spread across his huge face.

"It would be my pleasure gentleman," purred Hans staring angrily at George. "I do enjoy exterminating vermin. Just tell me where and when."

"We'll certainly do that. However, we have to ensure our plans are watertight. The walls have ears you know!" De Witt said looking at the Negro servants in the room. "We can't risk all our efforts to be sabotaged by our enemies."

Without warning, a glass shattering roar burst from the crowd, followed by the cacophony of spectators clapping and cheering hysterically, as George hit his one hundredth run.

"Hard luck Hans!" said De Witt. "You may have lost a thousand dollars now but just imagine the bonus you will get once you have knocked George for six."

The men stood up, as custom dictated when a batsman reached their hundredth run and clapped in unison. George turned, smiled reluctantly at the managers and raised his bat in acknowledgement of their congratulations.

"I'll soon wipe the smile of his face," raged Hans as he clapped slowly and mechanically.

"Temper your hatred," De Witt urged. "You must not show any animosity towards George and his acolytes. They must not suspect a thing. He is a romantic fool who has deliberatively thrown away his job, position and future. He deserves what he gets. We must plan carefully. We..."

"Darling!"

De Witt cut short his conversation, spun around and saw his wife standing at the entrance to the room.

"Deborah!" De Witt said in a surprised but angry tone. 'Who let you in here? This is members only and for men only! How long have you been standing there?"

16

After George clambered aboard the six- seater American Beechcraft Bonanza single-engine aeroplane, at Bartica airport, he noticed two empty seats at the rear of the cabin. Sitting down and taking a few ordnance- survey maps from his brown leather case he looked out of the window and saw dark, malevolent clouds looming in the direction of travel.

"Don't be scared Englishman."

George turned and looked ahead and saw Han's sunburnt, grinning, gargoyle face staring at him from the front of the plane.

"If you like I'll fly this bird," Hans said sarcastically drinking from a small, silver hip flask.

George ignored the German, settled into his seat, and started studying the maps in his hand.

"Anyone sitting here?"

George turned and saw Debbie smiling at him like a Cheshire cat.

"What are you doing here?" He said in a surprised manner.

"'Well it was either going to see the famous Kaieteur Falls or spend another day gossiping with managers wives about inane matters."

"Are you sure that's the only reason?" teased George replacing the maps back into his case.

Blushing with embarrassment Debbie sat herself down, smiled and nudged George gently in the ribs.

"Will you have time to show me around the Falls?" she asked placing her hand gently on his knee.

"If I can complete the survey in time and Hans doesn't trip

over his shoelaces and fall headlong into the river...maybe... also it looks like a storm is brewing."

George pointed at the dark, brooding clouds hovering ominously above them.

"If it's going to be dangerous why don't you do the survey another time when the weather is more conducive?" Debbie suggested opening her compact case and inspecting herself in the round mirror.

"Your husband wants the work to be done by yesterday! We are already behind time because of recent events."

Debbie closed the compact case and gently held his hand.

"Mrs. De Witt. I hope I'm not interrupting anything!"

Debbie quickly released her grip from George and stared at Hans who stood menacingly over the couple as if a vulture had cornered some carcasses.

"Your husband told me that you would be coming. I had saved you a seat next to the pilot so that you could enjoy the wonders of the Amazon rainforest, but I see that you are more interested in ..."

"Mrs. De Witt would love to sit up front," George interjected seemingly knowing what Hans was about to intimate.

"No thank-you, Mr. Schelling, I'm quite happy here. Also, I have a phobia about flying and need to sit as far away from windows as possible. I'm surprised my husband didn't tell you that. He's always informed the staff who were supposed to be looking after me about my condition so they would know what to do. I'll certainly remind him of his lapse in thinking when we return."

Han's face reddened and without replying walked slowly back to his seat fuming with rage that he had made a faux pas.

"I don't think he wants his boss to know that he hasn't followed instructions," said George nudging Debbie in her side.

"Never mind him," she said. "He deserves what he gets. He's a despicable man."

The sudden roar of the aeroplane's engine ended Debbie's conversation and she grabbed hold of George's arm tightly in anticipation of take-off. After a few seconds taxiing on the runway the American Beechcraft soared into the sky flying over the large expanse of mudflats and silty brown coastal waters on its journey to Kaieteur Falls.

"I hate flying," said Debbie as she tried to make herself comfortable in her seat. "And I especially don't like flying in this tin can."

'Why is that?" enquired George, smiling, as he unfastened his seatbelt.

"Don't laugh at me George," replied Debbie in mock anger. "Do you know what they call this flying bucket?"

"No, I haven't the foggiest my dear."

"The fork-tailed doctor."

"Why?" said George intriguingly staring deeply into Debbie's eyes.

"Because of the scores of crashes made by rich amateur, owner pilots."

"Well we will be safe,' he replied. "Our pilot is a professional and has over ten years flight experience with Bookers."

Despite George's attempt to comfort her Debbie stared at him with a worried expression on her beautiful face.

"Don't panic Debbie. We will be okay, I promise."

With his last words the aeroplane took a sudden nosedive as the tropical winds pushed up the aircrafts tail like a powerlifter throwing up a set of weights.

"It's not that," Debbie said in a quiet but clearly upset voice. "You know that my husband has suspicions about your involvement with Khan and the unions. Why get involved? Why jeopardize your future?"

George sat silently for a moment or two musing on Debbie's questions. Ali Persaud had told him the very same thing several weeks before and the news had forced him to be more circumspect in his dealings not only with Khan, but also with his work colleagues

"You know Debbie we all have choices. If you have a moral compass your choices will be steered in the direction of doing good...for doing what's right...for doing things without receiving a reward be that money, titles and even praise. What did Gandhi say? *You have to do the right thing...You may never know what results come from your action. But if you do nothing, there will be no result.* I want results even if it means I lose my job."

"But George, it's not that bad. At least the workers are not starving. They would be worse off without Bookers and Baillies' and the other plantation owners," she said looking earnestly at him.

"Have you heard of the eleven o'clock flog?" George asked quietly

Debbie shook her head.

"The eleven o'clock flog is when the workers, male and female are beaten by the overseers for not completing their work on time. It was supposedly outlawed several years ago but it still happens. That animal," he pointed angrily at Hans. "revels in continuing the vile practice."

George noticed a tear welling up in Debbie's eye but continued his tirade.

"Furthermore, you have heard what most of the overseers and managers do to the women they are interested in don't you?"

Debbie nodded, ashamed that she had indeed heard how white men had trawled for female victims on the plantation sites and once caught would lure them, on the pretext of love, money or goods, to an empty area of the plantation and proceed to rape and sexually abuse them knowing that no one would hear their terrified screams.

The pair of friends sat in silence ruminating on the conversation they had just had. George could tell by Debbie's demeanor that he had overstepped the mark by suggesting that she was ignorant of the history of British Guiana and the subjugation of the Indian and Negro workers. He looked at her trying to open her compact case with trembling fingers. He knew deep down, in his soul, that she wasn't the person to lecture on the pros and cons of life in this country. She wasn't the person responsible for the ills that befell the cane-workers and their families. She was

rather a kind,
considerate, empathetic strong woman who fought for the underdog. George felt thoroughly ashamed of himself.

"Look, I'm really sorry for haranguing you," he apologized whilst helping Debbie to open her compact case. "I owe you so much...without you I couldn't have helped the workers as I have done. You know that. I also know how hard you've tried to affect positive changes for all staff irrespective of their background. Please forgive me Debbie!"

Debbie shut her compact case, put it into her Lila hard case clutch bag and smiled at him.

"You don't have to apologize George. We are birds of a feather...we both have the same beliefs and values, But I'm worried for you."

"Why?" George enquired.

"I think you know why George!" Debbie looked deeply into George's eyes. "You know Subhan's death wasn't an accident. And you know you were followed to the meetings held at Uitvlugt and when Ali Persaud came to tell you..."

"Tell me what?" urged George.

"That Hans and some of the managers have been plotting to block your promotion because of your support for the workers. I think you are in danger George."

"Danger! What danger?"

"George. You can't trust Hans. He's capable of doing anything. He's been instructed to follow you."

"You knew?" George replied in disbelief.

"Only recently George. At the cricket match I overheard Hans and my husband talking...I only heard a little of their conversation but enough to understand that they didn't trust you. I was going to tell you. I promise you. I..."

Debbie stopped her conversation abruptly as she noticed Hans standing by her side.

"Your husband asked me to give you this," Hans said handing Debbie a small Leica camera.

George looked at Hans. He knew Hans didn't like him, but he

didn't realize to what extent. Now he seemed to understand why it had taken him longer than usual to climb up the rungs of Booker's career ladder even though his uncle was one of the most influential men in the organization.

"Guys can you please fasten your seatbelts. We're about to land and it might be bumpy," blurted the pilot as the light-aircraft descended into inclement weather.

After a few seconds of flying through thick, dark clouds, intense sunlight heralded itself into the aircraft cabin almost blinding George.

"It looks like the storm has blown away. Look," he said.

Debbie leant over him and peered down at Kaieteur Falls.

"Wow. It is magnificent," said Debbie pointing at the huge waterfall below. "I didn't realize how big it was. It's breathtaking."

"The width is 371 feet depending on the season and it has the longest single drop in the world...822 feet," added George.

"You are a walking encyclopedia," teased Debbie as the aircraft landed on the airstrip of the Potaro-Siparuni region of the Guiana shield.

Alighting from the plane George marveled at the spectacle before him. Although he had been to the region several times before, the wonders of the Falls and the surrounding rainforest and savannah ceased to amaze him. Kaieteur Falls was indeed one of the greatest wonders of the world he thought.

"I'm going to take some photographs of the area to be surveyed by Hans," he said. "Once I've finished, we'll have about half an hour to do some exploration together in more detail unless you have seen enough by the time we get back. The pilot does a mini tour of the Falls for about ten dollars if you are interested."

"Can't you show me something before you start? It looks like your co-worker is not in such a hurry as you are."

The two friends watched Hans, carrying a surveyor's box, saunter towards an Amerindian hut at the side of the airstrip. They looked as he sat on wooden bench, open up his box, pull out a bottle of bourbon and glass and proceed to drink.

"He's not going to leave for quite a while," laughed George. "Come on then. We'll walk to Boy Scouts view. It's about two hundred yards away."

As they walked across the sodden, lush vegetation the rumbling of the Falls could be heard in the distance. George led Debbie to Boy Scout's view, an imposing ledge which provided the onlooker with a unique, panoramic view of the cascading waterfall in all its glory.

"There is a God in Heaven," Debbie gasped in astonishment as she marveled at the waterfall in front of her.

"The old man's falls or as the Amerindian say Kayik Tuwuk Teur," explained George.

"This is divine. It's magnificent. Please take a photograph."

George took hold of Debbie's hand, led her near to the edge of the ledge and sat her down. As she prepared herself for the photograph Debbie noticed the date of 25.3.32 chiseled into the rock formation.

"Say cheese," George commanded as he photographed Debbie with his camera.

"Send me a copy when you have the photographs developed," she asked. "Oh and take a picture of this!"

Debbie was just about to pick a small brightly colored frog from one of the giant tongue bromeliad plants skirting the ledge when George sprinted towards her like a lion running after a gazelle.

"Stop! Don't touch it!" screamed George over the roar of the cascading Falls as he grabbed her hand away from the amphibian.

"You should have learnt about the wildlife in British Guiana. Especially the ones that might kill you!" panted George. "That small, beautiful miniscule frog you were just about to pick up is the Dart frog, one of the most poisonous creatures in the whole of British Guiana. It lives in this plant. Please promise me Debbie that

you will not touch any animal or pick any flower or plant without me being there."

"Of course, George. I think I've learnt my lesson well," she quipped rubbing her wrist which George had just grabbed.

"Look, I'll go and do my photo-shoot. Then I'll show you around the Falls. Why don't you go to the hut and have a drink and maybe you can suggest to Hans that he better start doing some work or your husband will not be that amused."

George watched as Debbie gingerly negotiated her way back to the airstrip hut. He then turned and headed into the rainforest skirting the Falls. As he trudged through the dense undergrowth of pink, yellowy bowl-shaped bromeliads, pink and purple orchids, bright green lichens, mosses and ferns, the scent of the Hoatzin or 'stink bird' wafted into his lungs via a warm breeze which made him feel slightly nauseous. Deeper inside the jungle he caught sight of a splendiferous orange colored fan-shaped crested Cock- of -the- Rock peering at him inquisitively from a liana which had entwined itself around a Kapoks tree. The bird's blueish black eyes constantly darted from him to something further into the forest and within a few seconds the plume of feathers on its crest stood to attention as it sensed a threat. Suddenly, and without warning the graceful bird took flight flapping its black wings over his head and disappeared deeper into the forest.

"You have a way of scaring away people and wildlife," Hans smirked, walking from behind a giant buttress rooted tree adjacent to the Kapoka trees.

"Have you started your survey yet?" George replied ignoring Han's malevolent glare.

"Survey? What survey?" Han's laughed as he put his surveyor's box on the ground and opened it. "I've come on a hunting trip and you are the prey. You English fool."

George saw Hans remove a semi-automatic Browning pistol from the box.

"Aah! The typical English upper lip treatment. You don't seem to be scared of death, do you?" said Hans pointing the gun at George's heart.

"Why should I be scared of you?" said George. "I killed hundreds like you in the war. Put it away and fight me like a man."

"Fight you like a man!" Hans roared with laughter forcing some blue and yellow macaws to vacate their nesting places. "Your no man...you left your wife all alone last year...she had a good time without you. Didn't she tell you? She met a real man!" With a demonic smile coursed across his face Hans made a sexually inappropriate gesture with his hips towards his adversary.

"What nonsense are you talking about?" George said in an irritated tone. "You've had too much to drink. Put the gun away, get on with your job and the sooner you finish the sooner we get home."

Hans waved the pistol teasingly at George.

"Oh, you naïve Englishman. Why do you think Mr. De Witt sent you to England for ten months? So you could get qualifications to rise up the corporate ladder? No, you fool. You had burnt your bridges once you started thinking of marrying that coolie bitch of yours."

George started to tremble with rage at Han's disgusting innuendoes.

"Yes. That's right Englishman. Now I've got your attention. You had no chance of getting the manager's job once you had refused to do as your uncle had requested and abandon that bitch. And you do know Mr. De Witt's predilection for nice young coolie flesh. Yes. He told me all about what he did to your bitch of a wife. She even enjoyed..."

Before Hans could finish his sentence, George lunged forward at the German but as he did so, the burly Indian man whom George had seen at Khartoon's roti shop and Subhan's funeral suddenly appeared in front of them and ran at him, knife in hand. George without thinking sidestepped the oncoming threat, karate-chopped him on the back of the neck and kicked the back of the Indian's left knee forcing him to the rain-soaked muddy ground. Hans knowing that George was too strong for his accomplice ran forward and kicked him fully in the stomach.

"Do you think I would be so stupid to come alone and try to kill you Englishman by myself when I can get someone else to do it?" Hans grinned looking down at his foe.

Winded, George gasped for air. Although Hans' kick had temporarily incapacitated him, his fight response triggered into life when he saw the Indian man lunge at him again with the knife aimed at his throat. Without thinking George grabbed his arm, twisted it one-hundred and eighty degrees and pushed it forcefully back into the into the Indian's midriff. The Indian's eyes widened in abject shock and pain as he gasped his final breath, slowly slipped to his knees and fell head-first onto the forest floor.

George looked up at Hans and saw the German aim the pistol at his head. Instinct and many years of army training kicked in and he scooped some wet soil and threw it into his enemy's face. With Hans temporarily blinded, he saw his chance to escape and ran headlong to the Falls jumping over roots of trees and fallen branches.

Suddenly, George heard a gunshot and immediately fell to the ground grasping his side. He looked down and saw a scarlet stain emerging from a bullet wound. He had been shot. Quickly the sensory receptors in his skin sent a message to his brain causing him to register the pain.

"It's just a flesh wound, Englishman," laughed Hans standing ominously over George and wiping the residue of wet soil from his reddened face. "If I wanted to kill you, I would have done so easily. No. I'll take up the offer of fighting you one on one!"

Hans threw his pistol behind him and with all the force he could muster, kicked George's wound. George stifled a scream of pain and looked at the blood pouring from his side.

"That's for all my comrades you said you murdered."

Hans lifted his leg and like a footballer about to take a penalty he kicked George squarely on the mouth causing blood to spatter over his boots and white socks.

"And that's because I hate you!" Han's shouted as he rubbed the blood off his footwear on some vines. "I didn't think it would be this easy."

Quickly, he grabbed George by the collar, lifted him up and threw him heavily to the ground. Images of Beebi, Steven, his parents and Liverpool swirled around George's head as he moved in between consciousness and unconsciousness. Slowly, his senses began to return, and he opened his eyes to reveal Hans' grinning, ugly face staring at him like a lunatic.

"Be ready to meet your maker," whispered Hans in George's ear.

From somewhere, unknown to George, an immense energy surged through his veins and without thinking he thrust his hips upwards and forced Hans off and onto the rainforest floor. George feeling the pressure on his chest and midriff subside rolled away from the German and he stood up holding his wounded side.

"I'm going to throw you over those Falls," smirked Hans pointing to the Falls some twenty yards away.

George knowing that his injury had placed him in a distinct disadvantage decided that attack was the best form of defence and rushed forwards, head- first at his adversary. Hans expecting such an attack braced himself and prepared to grab him in a bear hug. However, at the very last moment George lifted his head quickly and heavily into Hans chin forcing the German to step back and crash headfirst into the buttress of a tree. Seizing the moment George fought Hans like Heracles fighting against the ferocious Nemean lion. He punched Hans in the face with such a heavy blow that the skin of his knuckles ripped. However, Hans laughed at George's attempt to knock him over and he grabbed his arm and began to bend it backwards but George was his equal and quick as lighting he delivered a judo move which threw both men onto the floor but left him on top of the German. He punched Hans repeatedly in the face, but Hans lifted his knee and threw George overhead onto the edge of the waterfall. George looked down to the bottom of the abyss! Was this how he was to die, thrown off a cliff in the middle of nowhere? Gathering strength, he turned and began to wrestle

Hans. Both men grappled on the floor expending an inordinate amount of energy as each tried to strangle, punch and kick one another. Without warning George felt a pain shooting down his thigh and as he looked to see what had happened, he noticed blood coming from a tear from his trousers and Hans holding a small flick-knife. In the blink of an eye George seized the cold blade and began to turn it back onto its owner. But Hans was too strong, and he immediately forced the sharpened steel point back towards George's face.

"Now you die Englishman!"

Suddenly, Hans sat bolt upright as if in a trance and a trickle of blood began to course its way down from his ear. George quickly threw the German off himself and looked at Debbie standing behind Hans with a bloodied rock in her hand.

George stood up uneasily and took the rock from Debbie's trembling hand. Without a word he looked at Debbie and then at Hans who lay motionless as if in a deep sleep.

"Is he dead?" cried Debbie.

George nodded, looked at Hans and kicked him unceremoniously off the waterfall. The two friends watched as the German's lifeless, bulging body bobbed against the first ledge and then disappeared into the dark, vast, fast flowing Potaro river.

"Where did you spring from?" George gasped holding onto Debbie's arm.

"When I went to the hut Hans came and sat by me acting like the buffoon he is...was...and I noticed that his opened surveyor's box only had bottles of wine and a pistol. I though he was up to no good, so I followed him...at a discreet distance though."

"I'm glad you didn't listen to my advice. You saved me."

"But your wounded!" Debbie said pointing to George's side and thigh.

"They are only flesh wounds. I'll be okay. But didn't the Indian man see you following Hans."

"No," replied Debbie. "I made sure I was a fair distance behind Hans so he wouldn't think anyone was following him."

George stood silent for a moment. He realized that a lot of thought and planning had gone into Hans' failed assassination attempt but he also knew that he was not capable of organizing such a plan by himself. Only Hans, De Witt and himself knew of the work to be carried out at the Falls and the time scale involved. De Witt must have sanctioned the Indian henchman to arrive at the Falls before George and wait with Hans, at a pre-arranged time and place, to execute the plan.

"George, I knew you were in danger. But I didn't know that they wanted you dead,"

"Who?"

Debbie diverted her gaze from George.

"My husband, Wilde and Lloyd. As I said to you, before, on the plane...I overheard them discussing you at the cricket match. They said you were a liability. That's why I came today to let you know what they said. But I didn't know they would stoop so low as to try and kill you. You're going to have leave British Guiana as soon as possible. They'll be wondering what happened to Hans and why your still alive."

A myriad of thoughts raced around George's mind. What was Hans' trying to imply when talking about Beebi? Who else was involved in the plan to assassinate him? How many other people were involved in passing on information to De Witt and his cronies? Hatred and anger began to well in the pit of his stomach. His life had changed irrevocably. In a matter of minutes, he had become a wanted man whose life lay in the hands of the wife of one of his enemies.

"We'll tell the pilot that Hans will get the next flight," said Debbie. "And I'll arrange everything for your departure from British Guiana. The quicker you get out of the country the safer you and Beebi will be. Don't worry about your possession I'll get them shipped out after you have left."

17

"Please stop George! Stop! I couldn't prevent him..."

Beebi's face contorted grotesquely as George punched her in the face with such ferocity that her slim, nineteen- year old body-frame bounced backwards onto the greenheart wooden floor and concussed her.

George stood above his young wife, sweat pouring profusely from every pore of his massive, muscular body. He looked at his fist. His knuckles were red and the skin broken. He looked at the small bundle of life lying on the floor, motionless and pathetic. What had he done? What? He turned and threw the half empty bottle of Demerara rum he had been holding in his left hand onto the wall smashing the photograph of their wedding day. He looked at the picture through half opened eyes, the drink obscuring his vision. He could just about discern himself and Beebi standing smiling, hand in hand with the Kaieteur Falls behind them. He closed his eyes for what seemed to be an eternity and then raised his head slowly from his bull-like chest and tried to focus on the picture. The blurring subsided and he saw the rum run down the picture like raindrops on a windowpane. He turned and looked at Beebi and saw a thin line of blood trickle slowly down the corner of her mouth forming a disc pool on the floor. He fell onto his knees next to her, put his trembling hands on to his head and let out a heart-curdling scream.

"God! What have I done?""

He squeezed himself into a foetal position and closed his eyes. He squeezed and squeezed and squeezed. It was dark and warm and rushes of what seemed to be electrical impulses coursed through every cell of his body disabling him into a nothingness, a slipstream of ether that had no form, no mass, no past, no future, no present. He had collapsed into his own supernova. He was atman.

"Help, help me!" Beebi moaned as she lifted her arm limply off the floor and moved it languishingly onto the still body of her husband. "Help me, please!"

Feeling Beebi's touch a white light burned into every neuron of George's brain, scorching his very essence and jolting him back to existence as if he had been rescued from drowning.

"Beebi, Beebi!" He cried looking at her bloodied face as he cradled her in his arms. Tears rolled down his face into his mouth mixing with the rum to form an unholy alliance which seemed to bring him to his senses.

"I'm so sorry. So sorry," he cried piteously as he rocked his injured wife. "I'll never lay a finger on you as long as I live. Please forgive me!"

18

Liverpool, England 1973

Travelling to Lampeter, West Wales, would be one of the furthest journeys Steven had ever experienced since he was a toddler in British Guiana. Financial difficulties had precluded his father, George, from even contemplating the thought of a holiday to Wales, which was no more than one hundred miles away from Liverpool let alone boarding a plane to Spain, Malta or France which were holiday destinations that most Britons would head to after a year of saving and hard work. Steven had often felt envious in his early years when his best friend and next-door neighbour, Michael, left for foreign shores, with his family, every summer for six consecutive years from the age of eleven. Even more painful for Steven was the fact that he had to smile through the numerous recounts of his friend's adventures clambering up the volcanic mountains of the Canary Islands, diving in the Blue Grotto of Malta and cycling along the coastal paths of Normandy. Nevertheless, despite his unconscious jealously, he remained a loyal friend and confidant to Michael even until now, as he boarded the six- thirty morning Liverpool to Aberystwyth train.

"Have a safe journey mate," shouted Michael standing next to Steven's parents as the train slithered out slowly from Lime Street Station like a giant anaconda sliding into a murky, grey river.

Steven waved and stared back at his parents and portly friend, until they disappeared out of sight. Lugging a large, battered, blue suitcase which had carried his father's belongings to Liverpool seventeen years earlier, Steven manoeuvred himself down the narrow side corridors staring through windows looking for an empty compartment. After walking through two carriages, he finally located an empty booth. He slid the door open and hurled his suitcase onto the metal luggage rack above the dusty red, green, blue and white chequered seats. Steven sat and investigated his new surroundings. He looked at the two ceiling-mounted filament light bulbs located approximately a third of the way from the door, then gazed at the walnut panelling enveloping most of the compartments. Obscenities etched, by vandals, on the wooden frame around the window irked him. He put his finger into his mouth and, with a moist digit, tried to conceal the offending words. Content that he had been successful in bringing back perfection to the compartment soon evaporated into further irritation as the moisture quickly faded revealing the yellow lewd letters once more.

"You'll never get rid of them son. Don't waste your breath."

Steven turned around quickly to see a ticket collector smiling at him.

"The mindless idiots who did this, don't give a damn about anything. I'd reintroduce National service. I would. Yes, I would. Ticket please."

Steven fumbled into his beige Ben Sherman corduroy jacket and produced his ticket.

"Thank-you, young man."

The train official punched the ticket with his ticket machine, handed it back to Steven and exited without saying another word. Steven looked at his stub and a sense of wonder enveloped him. For the first time in his life he was doing what he wanted to do. He was embarking into the unknown and it felt great. The small, rectangular piece of paper he held in his hand was the passport to a new life and as he placed it back into his pocket, he smiled to himself contentedly. As he did so, he noticed a Liverpool Echo newspaper left on the seat opposite. The headlines screaming on the front cover read, *Home Loans. New Shock.* Steven was aware of how lucky he was to have secured a university place in these dark economic times as most of his friends were unemployed and his own family had to live on his father's low wages. His father. He felt a sudden pang of regret and self-loathing. His mind conjured up the image of his parents as they waved him goodbye from Liverpool Lime Street station minutes earlier. He had noticed that his father had recently lost a lot of weight, a fact made more apparent by the size of the jacket he was wearing. His father had always taken great pride in the made to measure Harris tweed jacket he had bought on his return to England, but now it ballooned around his body and made him look thinner than he really was. He knew that his father's loss of weight was not due to a deliberate dietary regime nor a debilitating disease but rather the result of poverty. Indeed, his father's wages barely paid for the mortgage let alone food and one thing had to give way. Unfortunately for the family it was food. The whole family had to survive on one main meal a day. Steven had thought it might be better if he had stayed in Liverpool and looked for a job to ease the financial burden of his parents, but his father was adamant that a university education was the best thing for him. So, with a heavy heart, he reluctantly took up his place at Saint David's University College, Lampeter knowing full well there would be at least one less mouth to feed at home.

As the train trundled on, he vaguely recalled the sunshine, fresh food, large detached house and swimming pool in British Guiana and compared them to the vivid images of a small, three bedroomed terrace house, limited food and darkness of his new life in England. His Liverpool home was freezing cold at the best of times, but winter pushed his family to the edge of despair. Several rooftiles had blown off the back outrigger and due to the lack monies his father had been unable to fix it, resulting in the bedroom ceiling collapsing. Worst of all this was his bedroom and he recalled the endless nights, when despite a hot water bottle placed under the bedsheets, he still had to sleep with his clothes on due to the freezing cold. At these times he wondered why his father had decided to leave British Guiana, but he had learned, early on in his childhood in Liverpool, that it was better not to question his father.

"It's none of your business! How dare you question me?"

Steven's seven-year old body trembled uncontrollably. His father had never hit him before and the shock of it had sent his world into overdrive. Pain, fear, incredulity mingled with aching love swirled around his mind and the whirlpool of emotions left him speechless and immobile.

"What are you doing George? What are you doing?" Beebi ran to her son and cradled him in her arms. "He's only a boy."

George stood above his wife and son, fists clenched, red-faced and unaware of what she was pleading. His gaze fixed on the two bodies in front of him.

"He's only a boy," repeated Beebi crying.

The movement of the larger body's mouth had no impact or impression on George's psyche. It was if he was watching a slow –motion recording where reality was suspended and replaced by a new dimension. George could feel a pounding in his head which was unbearable. Suddenly, he raised his fist and brought it down on the mouth that was moving. The contact of bone on bone brought him back to his senses and he stared at his wife's bloodied face and his son's eyes full of fear.

"He shouldn't give me back chat. Remember that!"

Steven recalled how his father had just left the room without apologising or making any attempt of reconciliation. What had driven his father to act in the way he did remained a mystery for many years and had left an indelible mark on him for the rest of his life.

Nevertheless, despite this haunting experience, Steven didn't hold a grudge against his father or even worse hate him. In fact, after days of consoling himself, and without an apology from his father, his love, respect and support for him grew stronger and remained unconditional. As time went by, he slowly pieced together the reasons why his father had changed from a loving, caring man to a man depressed, quiet and humourless.

Steven realised that despite providing his family with all that he could afford his father, since leaving British Guiana, had felt a failure. From being a man of considerable means with an important job, he had only managed to secure a menial position as a clerk with the English Electric Company. Finances were so tight that his father would often have to switch the electricity off in order to save money and resort in asking close relatives for second- hand garments to clothe his family. Steven also recollected the times his father had to swallow his pride and ask the local newsagent, rather than the bank officials, to cash his cheques because he had no disposable income left after all his bills had been paid. Living in poverty, Steven understood, was the primary reason for his father's angst and ongoing bouts of depression. In fact, from the age of seven the family home had become a house of tears, a house were laughter and sunshine had been usurped by sadness and darkness

As the train hurtled along to Crewe station, Steven began to feel weary and his eyes, heavy from tiredness, closed. Soon he was fast asleep and further images of Liverpool and British Guiana flashed in and out his mind. The heat of a Guianese day and the taste of coconut water by the dusty roadside of Essequibo merged imperceptibly with him playing football with his best friend, Michael, outside their homes in Liverpool. Quick as a flash he was transported to the front bedroom of his house where he saw himself crying because his parents were arguing relentlessly over money downstairs in the front parlour. Then in an instant he was back in British Guiana as a baby lying next to his mother but sensing that something ominous was about to happen.

"Penny for your thoughts."

Steven did not move or answer.

"Are you still alive?"

Steven, still somnolent, felt someone touching his shoulder.

"You were snoring mate. Loud as an elephant. Wakey, Wakey."

Steven slowly opened his eyes and gradually the form in front of him began to make shape.

"Chris."

The form placed its hand into Steven's and began to shake it.

"I bet your off to Lampeter."

Steven had gained full faculty of himself and looked at the figure in front of him. Short, stocky with brown hair parted to the left and wearing black rimmed glasses Chris could have been Billy Bunter's twin brother. He wore a red tie, black shirt. blue and white chequered jacket, black pin-striped, rayon trousers and Jesus sandals with white socks.

"Can I put my suitcase next to yours?"

Chris lifted his suitcase and stretched to reach the luggage hold. As he did so his jacket and shirt rose above his waistline revealing an unsightly white beer belly.

"God what have you got in your suitcase? Dumbbells? It's very heavy. Where are you from?"

"Liverpool. I'm Steven, nice to meet you."

"Ok wack," Chris smiled mischievously. "I'm only joking. I know you Liverpudlians are witty and like a joke."

Chris's ebullient smile and witty repartee made him immediately affable and Steven felt at ease with his fellow student.

"What are you studying at Lampeter?"

"How did you know I was going to Lampeter?"

Chris held up a train ticket stub and a packet of Anadin.

"You dropped these when you fell asleep. It says Aberystwyth. So, it's either Aberystwyth or Lampeter. I was hoping it be Lampeter and I was correct, wasn't I? And I hope you are feeling well."

Steven nodded and took his ticket and tablets and placed them back into his top pocket.

The train roared on past the flat fields of England and into the verdant rolling landscapes of Wales. Steven fell in and out of deep sleep despite the incessant chattering of Chris. Thoughts of his past rolled around his mind in time with the wheels of the train. Steven recalled his thirteenth birthday when he had wished to

receive a new shirt for his present rather than to be given his cousin's cast offs. So, he had hoped against all hope that on this special day he would receive a gift he wanted. However, when he opened his present and saw yet another one of his cousin's threadbare shirts, he threw it on the floor and ran upstairs screaming obscenities at his parents. To this very day he had felt a deep shame and regret for his outburst. Little did he know, at the time, what pressures his tantrum had placed on the shoulders of parents. Indeed, a week later they had given him another present and when he opened it and saw three new denim shirts, he was so elated that he hugged both parents enthusiastically. It was only a few hours later that he understood, to his eternal shame, what he had forced them to do. His mother had previously kept a picture of her grandmother in a solid silver frame on the mantelpiece. Soon after he received his present, he noticed the silver frame had been replaced by a wooden one. His mother had sold the frame in order to purchase the shirts. That night the guilt that he had made his parents feel fell upon him like a tonne of bricks and had preyed on his mind ever since.

19

Outside Aberystwyth train station, Steven and Chris waited patiently for the coach which was to take them to Lampeter.

"First Year students?"

"Yes," replied Chris.

"What are you studying?"

"I'm doing Theology and Steven's studying Geography."

"Oh no," mused Sean, the third -year student who had engaged the pair in conversation at the bus stop. "I wouldn't do Geography."

Steven looked at Sean. Over six- foot tall, skinhead haircut, good looking and athletically built, Sean looked intimidating with his red Doc Martens boots, drainpipe wrangler jeans and red t-shirt with a white peace sign emblazoned on the front.

"What do you mean?" asked Steven.

"If I were you two, I'd do Philosophy."

"Why?" retorted Chris.

"Because it's like water- easy to pass."

Sean started to laugh loudly as did his friend who stood by him, but until now had been silent.

"This is Mike-he's from Newcastle and he's studying Philosophy."

Mike was small, be-spectacled, black haired and overweight. He was dressed in grey Farah trousers, nylon blue jumper, white cotton shirt and black brogues. The two older students, Steven thought, looked incongruous together and he wondered how they had bonded initially for their friendship to last for three years.

"Let's go," Mike said and beckoned the rest of the group to get onto the coach which had just parked in front of them.

"Listen," Sean grabbed Steven's arm as Chris and Mike sat down on separate seats and whispered. "He's gay but he's alright. Is that cool with you?"

Steven looked at Mike and then at Sean and shrugged his shoulders in a noncommittal manner. What a question to be asked he thought. But as he sat down staring at the back of the heads of the two older students, he started to ruminate on the question. In fact, the more he thought about it the more he realised what an important question it was. Indeed, he had known that homosexuality was a taboo subject and that anyone found out to be gay, in his or others community, would usually, at best, be vilified and, at worse, get a hiding from ignorant males who, themselves probably, had latent homosexual tendencies. Steven was glad that he had been influenced by his parents' liberal views and his Sunday School's teachings' which enabled him to be non- judgemental and accepting of others irrespective of colour, creed, religion or sexual orientation.

"We've got about an hour to go before we arrive in Lampeter. I hope you brought your umbrella."

Steven turned and looked at Sean who was offering him a Wrigley's spearmint chewing gum.

"No but I've got my Kagoule. It rained when I came down for Fresher's Day."

Sean peered at Steven wistfully.

"Yeah...I think I remember you...last March wasn't it? You played squash and was having a deep conversation with my mate Bill in the Student's bar."

"The guy in charge of the Rifle Club," smiled Steven.

"Yeah...Bill said you were interested in joining if you managed to pass your exams. Well what a small world."

Sean turned, sat down and returned to his conversation with Mike.

As the coach cruised along the winding, narrow coastal roads of West Wales, Steven marvelled at the farms and green fields which rolled down to the beaches and merged into the Irish sea. The beauty of the scenic route brought a lump to his throat. He had

studied numerous books about the coastal geology of West Wales, as part of his sixth form dissertation, and now he could see the reality for himself in the form of the folded rock formations, deserted beaches and the famous coastguard lookout at Birds' Rock.

"We'll be in Aberaeron in a few minutes," said Chris. "Fancy a game of chess?"

Steven looked at the small wooded travel chess set that Chris had opened and lay on his black pin-striped trousers.

"I'm tired Chris. Maybe later."

Steven rested his head against the coach window and closed his eyes. He soon fell fast asleep and his head slid, side to side, following the movement of the coach as it meandered along the coastal road. Liverpool, his parents, his friends and British Guiana jumped loudly into his dreams replacing each other quickly and frequently. The memories continued to tumble over each other until Steven was rudely awaken by a shove in his shoulder.

"Steven. Wake up."

Through blurred eyes Steven recognised Sean kneeling on the seat in front of him again.

"Smoke?"

Steven saw Sean blow a white ring of smoke into the air from the joint he was holding.

"Not on the bus!" Steven replied almost apologetically. Although not a regular user of narcotics he did enjoy the mellowing effects of marijuana especially when dancing in the Babalou nightclub and Kirkland's bar in Liverpool's city centre.

"Don't be a nerd," laughed Sean. "No one's looking. Go on."

Steven looked at Sean then at the joint. Thinking that he would be offended if he did not accept the offer, he took the joint and inhaled. The smoke flowed into his larynx, then swam into his lungs and in a flash a relaxing sensation flooded into his brain causing him to feel euphoric.

"Yeah Man. Enjoy," Sean smiled. "There's plenty more if you want it. What about you Chris?"

Chris, without looking from his chess set, politely declined and focused on his game.

"Suit yourself," added Sean as he handed the joint back to Steven.

"Aberaeron. Anyone for Aberaeron?"

Steven listened to the coach driver and peered out of the window with the joint in his hand. He saw a small picturesque candy- box, fishing village with multi -coloured shops and a rectangular village green bordering the Irish Sea.

Several young men and women got onto the bus wearing black Lampeter Student rugby jumpers.

"Prynhawn da chi bastardiaid Saesneg"

The statement from a fat male student walking down the coach aisle didn't sound friendly especially when his two friends, who stood behind him, burst into a cacophony of sarcastic laughter.

"Croeso yn ol Sean my Saesneg friend! And you, you chi hyll gyfunrywiol!"

The vehemence of the remark was directed at Mike who blushed in embarrassment.

"Fuck off, you Welsh twat!" Sean shouted ready to attack the obese Welsh student who stood next to Mike.

For some unknown reason Steven grabbed hold of Sean's arm and persuaded him to calm down.

"Got a new gay friend. I didn't know you liked Pakis!"

Steven stared malevolently at the fat student. Heat and anger started to rise from the pit of his stomach and rushed to his brain. He clenched his fists until his nails ripped his skin. However, he wasn't going to rise to the bait.

"You there settle down or get off my coach."

The coach driver had slipped out his seat and stood squarely in front of the fat, racist Welsh student.

"Eistedd i lawr or get off. I mean it Alun."

Alun, the fat obnoxious student sat down at the back of the bus with his two friends laughing and speaking in Welsh.

"Just ignore him and stay clear of the rugby lot. If you have any problems let me know."

Steven winked at Sean and took another drag from his joint whilst staring, hatefully, at Alun.

A moment or two later, the coach continued on its way to Lampeter, via the winding A482 bus route and after about forty minutes driving along narrow tree laden roads past Fellinafach Theatre, Llanwennen and Creudynn Bridge the journey came to an end and the students alighted from the vehicle.

As Steven was about to set foot on the pavement outside the Black Lion Pub on the High Street, Alun barged past him knocking him and his suitcase to the ground.

"Watch where you are going Paki you ......"

Alun stopped abruptly as Steven picked up a revolver which had fallen out from his suitcase.

Silence and tension filled the air. Alun turned wan and achromatic and stood motionless like a statue. Fear had immobilized him.

"Don't shit your pants fatso," sneered Sean. "He's joined the Rifle Club and he has a license for the gun."

Alun and his friends grimaced at Sean and walked slowly away as Steven replaced his belongings and revolver back into his suitcase.

"You do have a license for that gun or isn't it real?" Sean asked jokingly.

"What do you think!" replied Steven smiling at his new friend.

20

Thomas Burgess and John Scandrett Harford had been instrumental in founding St. David's College in 1822 as a place of higher learning for Welsh ordinands. However, although initially established as a theological college, the late 1950s witnessed falling student numbers and as such the prospect of closure resulted in the College becoming a federal member of the University of Wales in 1971 and with it a change of academic subjects taught and a change in title to that of St David's University College.

The Old Building, which lay at the heart of the campus, had been designed by C.R. Cockerell to reflect and imitate many of the Oxford and Cambridge Colleges, and housed a bar, common rooms, administrative office, student accommodation, the old hall, chapel and library. Steven had been lucky in being allocated a room in the Old Building despite being a first- year student and as he stood outside his new residence, he marvelled at the Old Building's quad with its central fountain, Victorian lampposts and statue of St. David positioned above the glass doors which led into the chapel area.

After soaking in the atmosphere of his new surroundings Steven walked out, through two heavy arched wooden doors onto the manicured croquet lawns which faced a newly built library and arts complex. Turning left, he strolled along a gravel path, which skirted the lawns, and arrived at a set of concrete steps which led down to a car park, hockey pitch, three tennis courts and the narrow River Teifi which flowed gently through the campus separating the sporting pitches and academic buildings from four red- bricked halls of residence and sports hall which were situated on a gentle hillside on the other side of the river. After a few minutes of quiet contemplation, he continued his walk along the path which bordered the Old Building and arrived at the historic Norman mound which stood proudly adjacent to Lloyd Thomas Hall and the refectory.

"A can for your thoughts!"

Steven looked up in the direction of the mound and noticed Sean and Chris laying on the top with cans of foster's lager in their hands.

"Climb up, Scouser. We've saved you a can," Sean said with a huge smirk on his face. "Let's christen your first day at Lampeter!" Without thinking, Steven placed his hands on the base of the grassy mound and slowly clambered up until he reached the summit where his new- found friends lay. Standing in between Sean and Chris, he slowly turned three hundred and sixty degrees taking in the sights and sounds of the university campus. As a cool evening breeze brushed against his face, Steven inhaled the lemony scent of the countryside and stared at the hillsides bathed in the jasmine light of the evening sun. At this precise moment in time he knew that he had chosen the right university to attend and for that reason alone he could not have been happier.

21

Student life at Lampeter was much of what Steven had expected and more. He had indulged himself in all what the university had to offer during fresher's week, rag week in November, Christmas dinner and student ball in April. He had enjoyed room parties, disco nights, ice-cream eating contests at Conti's café, midnight walks to Lake Falcondale and playing for the university table-tennis, cricket and rifle club teams. Together with having a string of girlfriends from all year groups, he had become such a popular student that his circle of friends had widened beyond that of Sean, Mike and Chris. However, despite his positive bonding with fellow students and the town residents, he had not repaired the damage done with regards Alun from the rugby club. In fact, although many of his own friends belonged to the rugby club, a diehard group of Alun's sycophants would often harass him via racist name-calling and other disparaging innuendoes.

"Don't rise to the bait," Sean said as he placed a pint of lager in front of Steven in the union bar.

"I won't," Steven replied as he looked at Alun and his acolytes staring at him with malevolence in their eyes.

The student union cellar bar, in the Old Building, was small and compact. No more than fifty feet long and twenty feet wide, with one slot machine and one jukebox, the bar was the hub of the university where most students frequented. Seldom was there any form of violence in the bar save for the odd occasion when some townies would drink too much then deliberately start a fight with a student, usually one smaller than themselves. Students rarely confronted one another but recently National Front propaganda had been mysteriously appearing in students pigeon- holes together with insulting racist graffiti on students hall of residence walls, and as such heated arguments had risen between the extreme right wing members of the young conservatives and the rest of the students. It was no secret that Alun and his cronies were supporters of the National Front and Plaid Cymru and, for many left- wing members of the Labour and Liberal Parties, he was probably the chief engineer for the proliferation of racist messages in and around the campus.

Suddenly the lyrics from the band, Los Bravos, reverberated around the bar. Steven looked up and heard Alun and his motley group shouting the lyrics *black is black I want my baby back*, in an undignified, racist manner.

Steven's group ignored the obvious racial innuendoes when quite unexpectedly the music stopped in mid flow.

"Hey man I used to dig that song until you ragged it. Shit man! Ain't you got no respect for rock beat music?"

Standing in front of Alun and his rugby friends was Carlos Freeman. Six feet eight inches tall, two hundred and fifty pounds and black, Carlos made Alun and his group look like infants being scolded by a teacher. He dwarfed them with his presence and his verbosity.

"Hey what you doing singing that way? You got a problem with my skin colour dude?"

The group uttered not one syllable. They knew better. Carlos was an American exchange student from the Bronx, New York. He was a professional American footballer, granted a year's study at Lampeter, who had declined to play for the university rugby team as he had been offered a semi-professional contract with Carmarthen rugby club. Furthermore, gossip had spread amongst the university that he had killed two men in a gang fight when he was a teenager. Reputation apart, Carlos was the last person one would want to upset.

"You guys goin to behave or am I goin to have to have a workout?"

This euphemism was all that was necessary to persuade Alun and his rabble to put their glasses down and leave the bar in an ignoble way.

Carlos strolled to where Steven's group sat, pulled out a stool and sat down.

"Yo bro! Everything's cool now. I've met tougher women than them."

Everyone laughed, Carlos reminded Steven of Nimrod, son of Cush. Miss Mckenzie, his Sunday School teacher from the Anglican Church of St. James and St. Jude in Anfield, Liverpool, regularly referred to the stories of Nimrod from the Book of Genesis and the Book of Chronicles during her presentations. Nimrod was, according to Miss Mckenzie, a black man who was a powerful hunter and a man to be admired. Steven realised, years later, that his Sunday School teacher only referred to these biblical stories in order to bolster his confidence and self-esteem as she was fully aware of the racism facing him in and outside of the church.

"You guys shouldn't take any shit from them ...stand up and be men."

The group of friends laughed, but Steven knew that Carlos was right. He, himself, had stood up to bullies in Liverpool. Being of mixed race made him the butt of jokes, amongst his fellow and older pupils, from primary through to secondary school. But, on each occasion when he was physically or verbally attacked by bullies, he would fly into such a rage that he would fight with all his might leaving his tormentors bruised and bloodied. Unsurprisingly, after several years, Steven's reputation for being able to handle himself in fights led the bullies to sidestep him whenever they sought to intimidate other pupils. Steven knew his own strength but had no idea where the rage inside him came from and sometimes he would startle even himself when he saw the outcome of his temper. But since arriving in Lampeter he had deliberately put up with the racism and verbal aggression, of the likes of Alun, for fear of being unjustly accused of violent conduct which could possibly lead to university expulsion.

"We're not six foot eight and built like a brick shithouse," laughed Sean.

"It's cool," replied Carlos standing up and walking back to the bar. "But remember what I said guys ...man up."

22

The following day, after lunch in the refectory, Steven walked with Sean, Chris and Mike towards his room. As they opened the glass doors by the chapel and neared the fountain in the quad, Steven noticed a crowd of students and townsfolk milling around the library and arts complex.

"What's going on?" Steven asked.

"I haven't the foggiest," Mike muttered biting into an apple he had taken from the refectory. "Let's go and see."

The group of friends continued their walk and as they approached the path skirting the library, they stopped and stared at the commotion in front of them. Two large white vans with the letters HTV emblazoned on their sides were parked next to the Arts Complex and around twelve men, dressed in black t-shirts scurried around the area like ants, building a makeshift stage with cameras, microphones and broadcast equipment.

"Who are they filming?" Chris enquired.

"It must be them!" Mike answered throwing the core of his apple into a nearby bin and pointing to the side of him.

Steven looked over at three elderly men who were having make-up applied to their faces. He recognized Rees, one of the most vociferous Lampeter town councillors, but could not recall the names of the other two men although he knew that he had seen them before.

After several minutes, the makeshift stage had been erected and the three, elderly men sat down on wooden chairs which had been quickly provided for them. Steven scanned the crowd in front of him and saw many familiar faces both from the university and the town, but his gaze was drawn to several people standing behind the stage. Laughing and engaged in an animated, deep conversation with Rees was Alun wearing a white t-shirt with the words, 'Achul yr laith Cymraeg', written in bold black letters on the front and 'Save the Welsh Language' on the back.

"Oh, I remember now!" Sean said. "I read about this Plaid Cymru meeting on the posters that idiot Alun and his crew stuck up in all of the halls of residences last week!"

"I've not seen them!" replied Steven.

"Probably because just as soon as he put them up, they were pulled down even quicker by the left- wing elements of the student body."

The friends laughed. Steven recalled that throughout the year Alun had alienated scores of liberal minded students with his vile politics and intimidatory, bullying practices. Although Steven believed and subscribed to the notion of free speech and democracy, he couldn't undertand how people, such as Alun, despite all of the horrors of World War Two, still advocated hate and division rather than love and inclusivity. But unfortunately, in the here and now, Alun was in his element as he rubbed shoulders with likeminded individuals and the huge grin etched on his face was testimony to the fact that he relished every second of the limelight he shared with his associates.

After about five minutes, one of the three elderly men, who sat in the middle of the row, stood up and made his way to the microphone. As soon as he was about to address the crowd in front of him, Alun immediately led a chant of 'Plaid Cymru, Plaid Cymru, Plaid Cymru,' which was vociferously adopted by his fellow supporters.

"Diolch! Diolch! Thank you! Thank you! I am so glad to be here in this bastion of learning and this beautiful countryside town. I am so glad to see so many supporters of Plaid Cymru. So glad to see that the young and old of our communities are prepared to stand shoulder to shoulder in our quest for power. Firstly, to my Welsh brothers and sisters, please forgive me in addressing this meeting in English. There is method in my madness, believe me! As you can see, we have a diverse group of people attending this meeting together with a television company who will be broadcasting the length and breadth of our wonderful country. Therefore, I want my message to be heard and understood by everyone, Welsh speaking and non- Welsh speaking. My friends since 1925 when the 'Self- Rulers' and the 'Welsh Movement' joined forces to form Plaid Genedlaethol Cymru their primary aim for the party was to make the Welsh language the official language of Wales followed by Home rule. Have we achieved this?"

"No" shouted several supporters.

"No!" replied the elderly gentleman. "After nearly fifty years, we still have to beg the Conservative and Labour parties for support. But do they listen? Despite their false promises these two juggernauts of the political world do not have our best interest at their heart."

On hearing the impassioned speech, the supporters of Plaid Cymru shouted in unison 'Cynraeg I'r cymreg' and began to clap in unison.

"They woo us with false promises, on the eve of elections, but abandon us once they are in power!" continued the elderly man. "We, my friends, have to fight for our rights, fight for the maintenance of our language, fight for self-determination and fight for what is right. If we don't want our ancestral language to be lost, if we don't want to lose our cultural identity, if we don't want to lose our raison d'etre we must organize ourselves into a political machine which will devastate our opponents and secure our future. For if we lose our raison d'etre we lose our country. Is that what we want?"

Suddenly, from the corner of his eye, Steven caught sight of students holding placards with slogans written on them in red letters such as 'No to Nationalism', 'Democracy for Wales' and 'Vote Labour', exiting from the Arts Complex building. Immediately, on spying them, the cameramen and photographers swung their lenses in the direction of the counter demonstrators and the elderly man cut short his tirade.

"I think all hell is going to be let loose," whispered Mike.

As soon as Mike had uttered those prophetic words, Alun, red with rage, rushed towards his opponents pulling their placards down and pushing his fellow students onto the floor. Enraged with this deliberate, wanton act of aggression some counter demonstrators encircled Alun and hauled him against a wall. On seeing their friend incapacitated, several of Alun's group rushed to his aide punching and kicking whoever got into their way despite the impassioned pleading of the elderly gentleman for calm and peace. After several minutes of anarchy which was eagerly captured on tape by the HTV company, the high pitched scream of police sirens reverberated around the campus and within seconds police officers alighted from their squad cars and immediately began to corral and arrest the most violent of perpetrators.

"Should we intervene?" suggested Steven.

"No!" a bemused Sean replied. "We don't want to be caught on camera, otherwise we will be sent down from university."

"But look, Alun's punching a girl!"

Steven stared as Alun, despite being manhandled by a tall male student, threw a heavy punch onto the mouth of a thin female student, who was holding a placard, splitting her upper lip and causing blood to splatter onto his white t- shirt.

"I can't stand by watching this!" shouted Steven. But as he was just about to lunge into the melee to protect some students several policemen blocked his way.

"Stay back son or you'll be nicked"

23

"The University Senate managed to sort things out by offering a donation to the Town Council and Police funds. Alun and a few others got written warnings so the whole incident will be forgotten," Sean said as he took a swig from the bottle of cider he was holding.

"How do you know?" enquired Chris.

"I have my spies!" laughed Sean tapping his nose with his index finger.

"They got off lightly," replied Steven inhaling from a hash joint. "If this were a bigger, inner city university they would have gone down ...all of them. By the way how far is Mike's cottage?"

"About a half an hour walk. Just around the corner from Lake Falcondale."

"I'm looking forward to the party especially because of what happened during the protest two days ago. I need to relax," mused Steven.

Steven, Sean and Chris trudged slowly along the Heol LLyswen Lampeter road past the rugby club and local garage until they arrived at Forest road. Mike had organized a party in the semi derelict cottage he shared with two other students and had asked everyone to bring three things...alcohol, food and matches. Steven fully understood the rational for the former two requests but could not figure out the reason to bring matches.

"How long has Mike lived in the cottage?" Chris asked.

"Since Christmas of his second year. Although Mike enjoyed campus life, he disliked most of the refectory food. He hardly ate in his first year. Also, he's saving loads of money because the rent is so low," answered Sean.

Steven admired Mike. It took a lot of courage to decide to move away from the campus and live elsewhere he thought. The walk to and from the university alone would prove to be onerous to him especially during times of heavy snow and rain, both of which were common to Lampeter. No! Despite the food not being up to scratch, Steven knew which side of his bread was buttered...he couldn't sacrifice the warmth of his bedroom, hot running water for his bath, television and entertainment rooms and ultimately the union bar being only less than one hundred yards away for a rundown, isolated cottage.

The evening sun cast long shadows as the friends strolled through the verdant countryside. Steven looked up and noticed that the sky was red tranquility, its softness placated his soul and its warmth radiated his body creating a calmness which soothed his mind. He sucked in the air and it tasted sweet as candy floss. The fragrance from the summer grasses and flowers overpowered his senses and he felt as if nature had released all of its most appetizing aromas to entice unsuspecting visitors to its idyllic garden.

After walking for a further fifteen minutes the three friends reached a hairpin bend and spied Lake Falcondale, quiet and still, nestling amongst a regiment of conifers interspersed with alder, ash and beech trees. To the right, in the distance they spotted a small light emanating from a whitewashed building.

"That must be it there!" sighed Chris. "At last! My feet are killing me!"

The cottage stood lonely on top of a steep hill. The path to the building was overgrown with vegetation and broken roof slates and window glass littered its sides. Although it was bigger than he imagined, the cottage's dilapidated state worried Steven.

"It must be cold in winter," Steven said to his friends.

"It bloody well is! Especially when it snows. I've stayed there over-night and I froze my bollocks off!" Sean exclaimed as he knocked on the cottage door.

"You took your time," beamed Mike holding a bottle of Newcastle Brown Ale in his hand as he opened the door." What took you? Get in and get yourself a drink."

As soon as Steven crossed the threshold into the front room of the cottage hot air infused with the scent of incense sticks, marijuana, alcohol and burning logs enveloped him causing him to take a step backwards. Over forty students stood, sat and chatted to each other in the cramped small living space whilst listening to The Moody Blues 'Night in White Satin' record. Steven placed the aluminum foil wrapped baked potatoes he had been carrying down on a table and poured himself some homemade punch.

"Take it easy with that," laughed Mike. "It's not called a punch for nothing!"

Steven gulped down a mouthful of the alcohol and immediately started choking.

"What's in it," he gasped.

"Vodka, rum, gin and more vodka, rum and gin...with a touch of orange and raspberry juice!" Mike added with a smile on his face.

"I think I'll stick to the lager!" stuttered Steven wiping his mouth with the back of his hand and as he did so he noticed, standing next to him by the roaring fire, was the girl who had been punched by Alun at the protest meeting.

"Are you okay! I saw what that idiot did to you. He was bang out of order."

"Yes! Fine now. It's a bit sore," the girl pointed to her inflamed, split reddened upper lip. "I'll survive! Scars of war as they say."

"He's a coward and a bully. He should be thoroughly ashamed of himself," Steven added.

"Steven? Your Steven, aren't you? I'm Amanda nice to meet you."

"Yes. Do you want a drink?"

Without waiting for a reply, Steven poured the punch into a paper cup and handed it to her.

"Thanks. Anyway, we knew what we were letting ourselves in

for. Alun and his friends' reputation go before them. They are renowned for attacking anyone whomsoever might get in their way. But we won't be intimidated by them."

Steven was just about to answer when he saw Sean, standing next to Mike, waving at him from across the room and pointing to a joint he held in his left hand.

"Excuse me for a moment. I'm wanted."

Steven meandered his way around the students, in the middle of the floor, and reached Sean.

"Copped off again and in record time!" laughed Sean handing Steven the joint. "You are a quick worker!"

"No! Only talking about what happened with Alun," replied Steven taking a long drag from the joint.

"Amanda's really nice. She's a laugh but be careful. She has a reputation."

"What do you mean?"

"She's like margarine?"

"Margarine?" said Steven with a confused look on her face.

"Yes! Margarine. She spreads easily."

Shocked on hearing Sean's joke Mike gasped and spat out a morsel of chicken he had just eaten.

"That's really sexist, man!" joked Steven.

Sean was just going to reply when suddenly the music stopped abruptly, the lights went out and darkness invaded the solitary cottage.

"Don't panic!" shouted Mike. "Has everyone got their matches? if so light them now!"

Sound of students scrambling in their pockets and bags together with the sound of matches scratching boxes, broke the eerie silence and soon spots of small, oval shaped orange-yellow light pierced the blackness as if a midnight church candlelight service was being held.

Mike rushed to the kitchen and after about five minutes of tampering with the dodgy fuse box the lights of the house slowly awoke from its slumber and the music blurted out once more from the stereo system.

"Now I know why you wanted everyone to bring matches," Steven said smiling at Mike.

"Yes. There is method to the madness," said Mike. "But could you guys dot these around the cottage just in case it happens again. Light them as you go along."

Mike handed his friends around thirty candles and candle holders he had bought from the hippy 'Friendly Stores', based in Aberystwyth, some two weeks earlier.

"I didn't know we had to work for our drink!" laughed Sean as he went about distributing the candles around the house.

Whilst lighting one of the candles Steven spotted Carlos walking towards him.

"Give me a light bro!" Carlos asked with an unlit joint is hand. "I saw you at the demonstration. Did you get involved?"

"No! Not really! The police arrived and moved us on!"

"I know you don't like Alun, neither do I, but I must admit he's fighting for Welsh identity. I have to admire him for that."

"He could do it without threatening and attacking people!" Steven said, slightly annoyed at Carlos's intimations.

"You know the history of my black brothers in America," Carlos said inhaling from the joint. "We are not to dissimilar from the Welsh. We are a minority, our African language has been stripped from us, we are discriminated in all forms of society and we lack political power."

Steven watched as Carlos patted him on the shoulder, turned and shimmied into the middle of the room. Although the American's words resonated with him both on a philosophical and equality level his own gut feeling still made him feel an intense dislike, if not hatred, for Alun.

Three hours later Sean suggested to Chris and Steven that maybe it was time to get back to campus.

"But it's still black as Hades outside!" said Steven

"Are you scared?" Chris laughed.

"No! But I want to speak to Amanda before I go."

"You've lost out there," Mike said. "Look!"

Steven turned and saw Carlos gently kissing Amanda's injured lip.

"Never mind Steven lad. You can catch up with her some other time. Anyway, we have the match tomorrow. We need some kip! Let's get going," suggested Sean.

"See you tomorrow at lunchtime!" Mike said as he opened the door and watched his three friends enter the blackness of the night.

"I can't see a thing!" Chris moaned as he gingerly navigated himself down the hill almost tripping himself on the numerous long grass and weeds which infiltrated the path.

About one hundred yards away from the cottage the friends turned around and looked at the dimly lit building which they had just left.

"Should we go back?" Chris urged.

"No! We will be all right. Just be careful!" said Sean. "We are near the lake!"

The friends walked slowly and steadfastly through the lush undergrowth of the dark, brooding countryside each lost in their own thoughts. Steven looked up at the night sky. He witnessed an ocean of blackness peppered with silver specks of stars which seemed to wink at him sarcastically at every nervous step he took. Deep down in his soul he knew that the darkness had stolen his ability to navigate himself safely through the woodland paths. Fear began to gnaw away at him. He had never experienced such blackness before. He sensed that he was being watched and a shiver ran down his spine.

"Fuck what was that!" screamed Sean picking himself off the dew sodden ground.

"A root of a tree!" sighed Chris helping Sean up.

"We should have gone back!" said Steven.

The three friends stood and looked around themselves. Despite the stars, the blackness of the night engulfed them with fear and trepidation.

"Look! Through there! The lake," whispered Sean.

The friends looked in the direction he was pointing and saw a black watery mirror with starlight shimmering on top.

"Lake Falcondale! Come on we'll find the path in no time!" Sean continued gleefully.

Several minutes later the friends arrived at the lake, whose face was as smooth as black glass, and stood on the path that circled it. The only sounds they could hear were the soft whispering of trees blown by a cool breeze.

"We just need to keep on the path and then we'll be on the main road" said Sean. "And take a puff of this! It'll calm you down!"

Sean handed a newly lit joint to Steven who took it and inhaled deeply.

"Your turn ChrIs! Go on you look exhausted! It will help. Believe me."

Despite his views on drug taking, Chris, considering all that he had just gone through, took the joint, placed it between his lips, looked at both Sean and Steven and inhaled. Immediately he started to gag and threw the joint onto the floor.

"Hey, don't move," instructed Sean as he slapped Chris gently on the back and bent down to retrieve his joint.

"What was that?" he said as he straightened up.

"What was what?" asked Steven.

"Didn't you hear anything?"

"Hear what?"

"The noise from over there!"

Sean pointed to some conifer trees further down the path.

"Stop pissing about Sean," said a startled Chris. "I'm already frigging scared!"

"No seriously. Didn't you hear anything at all?"

Steven and Chris shook their heads.

"Must be the joint then. It's making me paranoid. Come on let's get going."

The friends continued their journey until they saw blobs of light, dancing in the darkness in front of them.

"We are near the road...look there's some cottages," Sean stopped talking and beckoned his friends to be silent.

"Did you hear that?"

"Hear what?" replied an annoyed Chris. "Stop messing about. It's bad enough that I can hardly see where I am walking without you scaring the shit out of me!"

"But I'm sure I heard voices."

The friends stood still and looked in the direction of the cottages.

"I can't see or hear a thing," Steven whispered. "Are you sure you are not hallucinating?"

Before Sean could answer Steven, a rustling of foliage, crack of twigs and splash of water was heard by everyone.

"It must be water vole or beaver," suggested Chris. "Come on let's get out of here!"

The friends quickened the pace and within moments they had reached the road which led back to the university campus.

"Phew! Don't ask me to go on any midnight walks ever again," Chris moaned.

"Look I was right after all," shouted Sean.

Ahead of them, no more than twenty yards away, three shadowy figures stood spray painting the front of one of the white cottages. On hearing Sean, the figures turned towards him, stopped what they were doing and jumped into a waiting car which was parked, engines running, on the other side of the road and sped away in the direction of Lampeter town.

On arrival at one of the cottages Steven read the words 'Wales for the Welsh' crudely written in green, red and white spray paint.

'Did you recognize any of them?" asked Chris gasping for air.

"No...but I'm certain that the car was a ford escort," replied Steven

"And you know who owns that car don't you!" smirked Sean

"Who?" Steven and Chris asked.

"Your mate Alun!" answered Sean with a sly grin on his face.

24

Television pictures of the recent demonstration on the Lampeter campus together with the news that English owned cottages had been targeted by Welsh Nationalists were the topics of conversation amongst the students throughout the university. Tension between the left -wing and right -wing activists had reached such a fever pitch that the President of the Union and Chancellor of the University had suggested an extraordinary union meeting to redress the situation.

The unusual, hostile atmosphere pervading the university was felt deeply by many including Steven as he sat with his friends in the refectory during lunchtime. He noticed that Alun's group of friends had been joined by scores of Welsh speaking students creating a discernible English-Welsh divide.

"Things must be getting bad," said Sean. "It's the first time I've seen Rhodri sit on the same table as Colin and his idiots. Although Welsh, Rhodri's a liberal at heart."

"I wonder if Alun has been coercing him," Steven suggested pouring himself a cup of coffee.

"I hate politics," groaned Chris as he lifted a large metal milk jug. "It causes so much division....and that's just great no milk left!"

"Don't worry I'll get you some more," Steven said as he stood up and walked towards Alun's table which had four milk jugs stationed on top.

"Here take this one!" snarled Alun pushing a jug towards Steven.

Steven picked up the jug and looked inside. Swimming on top of the milk were several large yellow- green pieces of snot. Steven's stomach churned over and he felt as he was going to vomit.

"Go and drink it! You'll need your strength for the match!" laughed Alun looking at his cronies.

Steven looked at Alun in disgust but fixed his stare on Alun's fingernails as he took a mouthful of soup.

"I didn't know you painted your fingernails! Getting in touch with your feminine side?" smiled Steven

Alun threw his spoon violently into his bowl of leek soup and in doing so he saw the red, green and white paint which covered the tips of his fingers.

"What do the colors represent?" continued Steven sarcastically.

Angered and belittled, Alun stood up and pushed his bowl off the table. The noise of the bowl smashing onto the floor forced all of the students, lecturers and waitresses eyes to fall on the two warring young men as they stood in a sinister Mexican Standoff. Alun was just about to scramble over the table to attack his foe when he caught sight of a History lecturer, Mr. Mackay, staring at him from the dining table from which the university academic staff ate. Sensing that he would be making a noose for his own neck, Alun sat down and scowled malevolently at Steven.

Without a word, Steven replaced the jug on the table and, staring at Alun, picked up another one and took it over to his friends.

"What was that all about!" enquired a concerned Chris as he buttered a slice of bread.

"You don't want to know!" replied Steven pouring milk into Chris's cup. "And remember not to stuff yourself too much. We have the match to play remember."

Several hours later the Sports Hall was crammed with around one hundred students waiting in eager anticipation to either watch or play in the annual five-a-side football tournament.

"Are we all here?" asked Sean as he distributed yellow t-shirts with the words, 'On the Grapevine', written in red on the back and an image of a bunch of purple and green grapes on the front to Steven, Chris, Mike and Carlos. "You guys can pay me back later!"

The small changing room was crammed with players putting on their kits and Steven was glad that he had got ready first as he opened the door and stepped into the corridor.

"Good luck!" shouted Amanda standing by a staircase which led up to the viewing balcony which overflowed with fellow students.

"Steven boyo. Come here please!" shouted Dai Davies, a theology postgraduate student and organizer of the football tournament.

"Your team is first on. 'On the Grapevine' versus the 'Bellenders'. It's an eight- team knockout competition. Fifteen minutes each half. You all know the rules, don't you?"

Steven nodded, opened the changing room door, and looked for his team players.

"Come on lads. We are playing first!"

Pushing open the door to the football pitch, Steven's heart sank. In front of him, kicking a ball to one another, was Alun and his teammates.

"Look who it is!" Alun said sarcastically to his friends.

They all turned in the direction of their opponents and laughed hysterically as Alun made a disparaging comment about Steven.

"Captains!" commanded Dai. "Can you come to the center circle please."

Alun and Steven walked slowly across the sports hall and stopped in front of Dai.

"Right! You both know the rules. Let's have a good game. Good luck to you both. Shake hands please!"

Steven reluctantly lifted his hand towards Alun who immediately grabbed hold of it and started to squeeze it hard. Although in pain Steven did not display any emotions and merely glared deep into his Welsh opponent's eyes.

"OK, OK! That's enough!" Dai said pulling their hands apart. "On the Grapevine to kick off!"

Turning to his team, Steven winked, placed the ball on the center of the circle and on hearing Dai blow his whistle passed the ball diagonally to Sean, who had raced forward on the right. On receiving the ball, Sean immediately ran with it for a few yards before passing it across to Steven who had made a forward run. Despite one of the opposing team members attempted tackle, Steven flicked the ball into the air, chested it down, dribbled past another oncoming player and toe-ended the ball into the corner of the opposition net for a goal.

"Great goal!" shouted Sean as he and his teammates encircled Steven and patted him on the back. Steven looked up at the balcony and felt immense pride as he saw lots of students celebrating his goal by banging on the window.

With the ball replaced on the center circle and whistle blown Alun booted the ball sideways to one of his players. However, Steven anticipating such a pass intercepted the ball and side-footed it to Mike who quickly kicked it into the path of Sean. On seeing this Alun, already angry for going one goal down, charged after Sean and deliberately kicked and tripped him from behind causing him to career, headfirst, into a side wall.

"Referee!" shouted Mike enraged with Alun's malicious foul.

After blowing his whistle and admonishing Alun with a yellow card, Dai walked towards the injured player. Sean, clearly dazed and bloodied placed the ball down for a free kick. As his teammates rushed forward into the 'Bellenders' half, he quickly flicked the ball to Chris who back heeled it to Steven who then instinctively volleyed it past the flailing goalkeeper into the top left hand corner of the net for a second goal.

Once again, a tumultuous roar emanated from the crowd on the balcony as Steven's 'On the Grapevine' team jogged back to their own half.

When the game was restarted for a third time Alun, fueled with rage, dribbled the ball skillfully past Chris and Sean and was heading straight for goal when he saw Mike running to tackle him. Quickly he trapped the ball with his left foot and as Mike slid in to make an interception Alun booted him directly in the testicles forcing Mike to scream in agony.

"Bastard!" shouted Sean.

On seeing Sean running to attack him, Alun threw a right hook which caught his opponent flush on the temple sending him backward onto the wooden floor. Steven boiling with anger, ran then jumped into the air and landed a flying karate kick on Alum's nose which sent Alun crashing onto a wall. Suddenly all hell let loose as each player, from both teams, started brawling with one another despite Dai's protestations. About a minute into the mass fight the Sports hall door opened, and four porters ran into the hall to separate the warring factions.

Inside the changing room both teams, separated by the porters, stared malevolently at each other whilst nursing their bloodied faces and injured limbs

"You all know the rules," Dai said. "You've let me down. You've let yourselves down. You've let the university down. I have no option to disqualify both teams and you'll have to leave the building as soon as possible."

Mike started to remonstrate blaming Alun and his team for the debacle, but Dai refused to listen and exited the changing room without saying another word.

"You're a bastard!" screamed Mike at Alun.

Alun said nothing, unzipped his Gola bag, took out a white towel and wiped his bloodied face.

"Your responsible for this!" continued Mike. "You've spoiled it for everyone!"

"Fuck off Quentin Crisp, you faggot!" roared Alun as he threw his bloodied towel into Mike's face.

Steven quickly picked up the towel and rushed forward to flick it at Alun when suddenly Porter Owen caught him by the arm.

"Calm down. Calm down. Steven boyo. It's not worth it."

As Porter Owen loosened his grip, Steven threw the towel at the feet of Alun and as he did so he noticed several spray cans and brushes in the Welsh student's bag.

Alun looked down at what Steven was gazing at.

"Nosey bugger," snarled Alun as he covered the cans with his towel.

"Look lads get your things and well get changed back in my room," Steven said to his teammates.

Outside the Sports Hall Steven and his friends descended the steps and headed across the bridge towards the tennis courts.

"Guess what I saw in his bag?''

"What?" said Sean nursing his cheek.

"Spray paints! The same colors which were sprayed onto the cottage walls."

"Great we've got evidence that the bastard's been defacing buildings. We'll have to tell the police and the University Senate," Mike added.

As the friends reached the steps that led up to the library, Steven stopped and looked in earnest at his friends

"Although I dislike Alun and I despise his politics. I've been brought up not to be a snitch. I can't bubble him up. He'll fall on his own sword one day. Mark my words!"

25

Days flew past and soon Steven had finished his last Geography exam. Education had been the last thing on his mind, and he felt guilty as he put the lid on his Parker fountain pen and placed it back into his blue wrangler shirt pocket. What would his parents think of his antics during the year? To all intents and purposes, they thought he was working hard and to his best ability every day. Little did they know, he pondered, that he had only attended lectures in the first month and had not read any books on his booklist. On the contrary he had partied, womanized and relied on Brodies and Coles notes to try and pass his first-year exams. Well, he thought, nothing could be done about it now. His only hope was that he would scrape forty-five percent in each exam which would see him safely into the second year.

"How did you do?" asked Chris as they walked out of the main exam building into the summer sunlight.

"As well as you," laughed Steven knowing that Chris had done as little studying as himself.

"Never mind," smiled Chris hugging his friend by the neck. "Coffee at Emlyn Evans?"

Steven nodded.

As the friends walked past the tennis courts and up the steps towards the library on the way to the café, which was situated on Bridge Street, Steven saw Alun and his cronies approaching them.

"Hi Paki! Failed your exams?"

Alun's disparaging comment cut through him like a knife

through butter. Steven felt belittled, sick to the stomach and tensed up with fury.

"Leave it," urged Chris. "Don't listen to the prat."

As he said this to his friend, one of Alun's thugs shoulder barged Steven spinning him around.

"Watch it," Chris shouted.

Without looking back Alun and his gang roared with laughter and continued walking towards the hockey pitch.

"That idiot's going to get his block knocked off one day and I hope I'm there to see it. Are you ok?" Chris asked.

Steven said nothing. Fire raged in his veins. Neurons charged around his brain as fast as the speed of light and although his amygdala switched into fight mode, another part of his brain whispered to him to remain composed and not rise to the bait. After several minutes, the friends reached Emlyn Evans. Steven pushed open the door to the café and noticed Sean sitting alone at a table.

"Where were you?" asked Chris, "How did you do in your exam?"

Sean took a sip of his milky coffee and wiped his lips with the back of his hand.

"Well my dear friends," Sean paused for a moment before continuing. "I've deferred."

"Deferred?" quizzed Steven.

"Yes deferred. That means I'm going to have to do my finals next year."

"You mean you're going to do four years instead of three?" Chris exclaimed.

"Either that or fail my exams. You know I've not studied this year. This way I get another chance to get stuck into some learning."

"You are not going to study next year either," grinned Chris.

"At least I won't be kicked out, and my parents won't go ballistic," replied Sean biting into an egg and bacon sandwich.

"Here are your sandwiches. I've just made them. I knew you'd be in around now," said Blodwyn, a sixty-year old waitress who had taken an immediate liking for the group of friends, especially Steven.

"How's my favourite Einstein then?"

Steven blushed and smiled at his admirer.

"Here you go my lovely. And an extra piece of toast for you Steven."

As Blodwyn topped up his cup of coffee, Sean and Chris tried hard not to laugh whilst kicking their friend playfully under the table.

"If you ever wanted a wife, she's more than willing," chuckled Sean as Blodwyn left to serve another customer.

Steven was just about to chastise his friend when the bell of the cafe door rang and a family of three entered. Steven's gaze was directed past the older man and woman to that of a young girl, about his age, dressed in tight blue drainpipe jeans and a yellow, tight fitting t- shirt. To Steven the young girl was beauty personified. He stared at her long straight black hair, tied at the back with a red ribbon, marvelled at her clear light brown complexion and high cheekbones, impressed at her hour- glass figure and felt stupefied by her dazzling opalescent green eyes.

"Wow! I haven't seen her before," whispered Chris.

"Nor I," Steven replied.

"Are you in love?" smirked Chris with a piece of bacon wedged between his front teeth.

"Shh!" whispered Steven as he nudged his friend with his elbow.

"She must be an overseas student," Sean said.

"How do you know?" Steven asked.

"Every June, overseas applicants are invited to view the university. Some of the families reside in Lloyd Thomas Hall or the Old Building for a couple of weeks or more so their kids can decide if they want to stay or not. I've seen some Italians and Chinese families on Market Street today. If you're interested, I can find out which room she's staying in from Porter Owen."

Steven said nothing. He kept gazing at the beautiful girl who sat sandwiched between her parents and as he did so, he fiddled nervously with his spoon.

"I said I can get the number of her room for you," laughed Sean grabbing hold of Steven's spoon and interrupting his friends love thoughts.

"I don't know," smiled Steven embarrassingly. "She might think it creepy that I know where she lives before we've even been introduced."

"Don't be silly," interrupted Chris munching on a piece of egg. "It's not that you are actually going to knock on her door as soon as her mother and father have left? Is it? No! You just have to hang around there and accidentally bump into her...not literally I mean. That would be creepy! Just wait for her to come out of her room and say hello."

Steven ruminated on Chris's plan and it did indeed make sense to him. He knew that there would be a queue of hot- blooded, male students wanting to date the new girl, but he wanted to be the one and only suitor. For the first time in his life he had felt love, not lust. Here was his soulmate. Here was his destiny. Here was his love of his life.

"Could we try three of your cream teas? I believe they are the best in this wonderful town," the father of the young female asked, smiling at Blodwyn.

"They certainly are my darling and may I ask where you have come from?"

"Amsterdam. My daughter may be starting at the university this term."

"I've always wanted to go to Holland, my dear," interjected Blodwyn. "I'd love to take a ride along the canals and visit the tulip fields. As for your daughter she'll love the university. Everyone is friendly."

"She is a student." whispered Chris.

Steven ignored his friend and sat mesmerized looking at the young girl.

"Are you in love?" Sean asked sarcastically.

Just before answering, Steven caught the eye of the young girl and for a moment, which seemed to be an eternity, they stared at each other as if they were connected as one.

"He is in love," Sean and Chris echoed together.

"Keep it down lads," an irritated Steven replied as the father of the young girl looked around at the group of friends.

"He heard that," continued Steven. "Let's pay and go. You've embarrassed me enough, you nutters. And don't say anything when we leave."

The friends rose, waved goodbye to Blodwyn and exited the café.

"Quick," shouted Steven to his friends. "Let's go to the Porters Lodge and find out which room she's staying in."

The three friends ran to Harford Square, hurtled past Midland Bank and turned right through the university gates to the Porters lodge which was a mere two minutes away from Emlyn Evans cafe.

As the group burst through the door Porter Owen, a portly small man in his mid- fifties held his finger to his lips.

"Don't tell me Boyo. You've come to find out where that new lass is staying?"

"How did you know?" laughed Steven.

"Well I did sign her in this morning and give her the keys to her room. And by the way two other students have asked the same question after they set eyes on her. Mind you, boyo, I don't blame them. She is a stunner. Not may coloured girls like her around these parts you know."

"Who were they?" replied Steven in an annoyed tone.

"What's it worth boyo?" joked Porter Owen covering the signing in book with his hand.

"A pint in the union bar," said Sean.

"That'll do fine boyo. Alun and his rugby friend Andy first saw them when they arrived."

Steven's irritability began to bourgeon at the answer. The very thought of Alun trying to seduce the new student filled him with an enmity which surprised even himself.

"Where's she staying Porter Owen?" enquired Chris.

"In Lloyd Thomas hall, ground floor room 6a, next to the laundry room. There was no room in the Old Building."

26

A few days later Steven was drinking with his friends in The King's Head, the smallest, most intimate pub in Lampeter where both students and locals drank without fear of trouble. The interior of the pub reminded him of several pubs back in Liverpool where traditional bar games still existed such as bar skittles, shove- a- penny and darts. Sitting at the bar with Chris and Mike, he stared, unconsciously, at Dewi, the pub owner. Dewi was a local hero in Lampeter and the surrounding district. A former World War Two fighter pilot, he was the only airman from the village to return home alive. Unfortunately, he had not been immune from the horrors of the war because his Hurricane fighter plane had been shot down by a Messerschmitt over the Dover coast. Although Dewi had managed to parachute from his plane his cockpit had become the head of a blowtorch and the ensuing fire had engulfed every inch of his body. Miraculously, he survived the crash but not without horrendous life changing injuries. Besides being severely burned all over his body, his eyes were now no more that slits and his nose had been all but destroyed. According to his friends, as the publican seldom reminisced about his war days, he spent the rest of the war as a 'Guinea Pig' in the Queen Victoria Hospital, East Grinstead where reconstructive surgery was conducted on his badly, burned face. Steven looked at a photograph of Dewi, before the outbreak of the war, hanging next to the spirit bottles and thought what a handsome man he had been in his youth. But as Dewi handed a pint of Guinness to him the full horror of war was made abundantly clear. Dewi's face was disfigured and discoloured to such a decree that he now understood why numerous pubgoers, on certain occasions, refused to imbibe in the King's Head on the grounds that they couldn't bear to look at the publican's face and drink at the same time.

"Stop staring."

Steven's eyes followed the contours of the pink, purple and red lines that etched across Dewi's face like that of a London Underground map.

"Stop staring."

This time Chris pinched Steven out of his hypnotic stare.

"Sorry, miles away."

"I know...I'd thought you'd be fixating your thoughts on the girl you saw in Emlyn Evans a couple of days ago rather than on Dewi's face!"

Steven took a sip from his pint and rubbed the white froth from his lip with the back of his hand.

"I've seen her a couple of times but not had a chance to speak to her."

Chris looked at Steven quizzically.

"Okay! I didn't have the bottle to speak to her. I admit it," said Steven.

"But you are a Lothario! You've never had trouble chatting to girls before," replied Chris sipping his pint of lager. "What's up with you?"

"I don't really know. I just feel inadequate every time I see her. It's as if she's too good for me. I can't even bear to see friends in Lloyd Thomas because she's staying there."

"Well I've got some good news for you on that point."

"What do you mean?"

"Well my spies have found out two things about her."

"What?"

Chris lifted up his empty glass of lager and shook it in front of his friend. A smile spread across his face when Steven ordered another pint for him.

"Ok. Spill the beans."

"Her name is Anna and she's starting immediately."

Steven took another sip from his drink.

"Oh, and another point."

"Yes?" said Steven.

"She's studying Geography and will be in your class for the rest of the term."

"Your joking."

"Moi. Non," laughed Chris.

Suddenly the front door of the pub opened, and Sean entered in a high state of frenzy.

"Steven! You better go to the Porter's lodge right away there's an important call from you mum. Get going man!"

Steven looked at Sean then at Chris and Mike. He grabbed his wrangler jacket and ran out of the pub wondering what on earth was wrong.

27

Three days later and Steven was still ensconced in his room. He had ignored the knocks on the door from his friends and had even refused the cleaner into his room. The phone-call he had received from his mother a few days earlier had devastated him. His beloved paternal grandmother had died and despite his pleadings to his mother, she was adamant that it would be better for him to say at Lampeter rather than travel to Liverpool for the funeral. Although his friends would think it odd that he would not attend a close relatives funeral, he knew why his mother had persuaded him not to. Two years earlier his paternal grandfather had died suddenly from a heart attack. The death itself didn't seem, at first, to have had an adverse effect on him but, at the funeral, he had broken down to such a degree that he suffered severe headaches for several months after, resulting in him being administered Anadin. Now it seemed history was repeating itself. Anadin wrappers littered his floor together with empty bottles of Thunderbird wine and cigarette butts.

Steven stared at the ceiling. A dull pain sat at the front of his brain and weighed him down. His sinews stretched tight. Teeth clenched, he gripped the sheets tightly to his neck. Black, suicidal thoughts ebbed and flowed through his mind like the oceans on a moonlit night. The more he thought, the more he was engulfed by fear and guilt. Why did his grandmother die? Why hadn't he spoken to her for weeks? Why was he so selfish? What must his father be thinking? Steven lay sweat-soaked on his bed impervious to the world.

Suddenly his thoughts were interrupted by loud banging on his door.

"Steven. Steven. Steven! Are you okay?"

There was no reply.

"Steven. Let us know if you are ok mate."

Chris's pleadings were not reciprocated.

Steven loosened the grip from his bedsheets. He threw an arm out towards the bedside table and groped for the glass he had filled with Thunderbird wine. Eyes closed and hands trembling he gripped the glass tumbler. Steven forced the glass to his lips and took a huge sip of the fortified wine. He gasped almost immediately and spilled the rest of the drink over his face, chest and bed linen. He scolded himself and threw the glass violently against the floor.

"Steven. Are you okay? Open the door."

Steven lay on the bed and ignored his friends' supplications.

"Ok mate. I've heard the bad news. I'll give you a call later."

Steven listened as his friend's footsteps disappeared down the corridor of the Old Building. Alone once again, he hauled himself out of bed and walked to the sink. He took his member out and urinated into the bowl. He watched as his pee disappeared down the plughole leaving yellow droplets on the side of the white basin. Slowly, he looked up to the mirror and switched on the light. He looked at himself. Stubble covered his chin, his eyes were red as tomatoes and his face ashen. He knew he was unwell, but the demons had returned. Inside his head a voice repeatedly chanted *kill yourself, kill yourself kill yourself*. He watched the sweat pour from his forehead onto his face creating rivulets amongst his stubble. He felt his hand raise and move towards a razor which lay next to an unopened bar of soap. The voice, mocking him, grew louder and told him to place the razor against his throat. Steven hypnotized by the voice stared at himself in the mirror. His fist held the razor tightly, his knuckles reddened, and his arm shook. The voice began again. *Kill yourself. You know you want to release yourself from this pain. Go on. You have the power. Be brave. Be a man. You have the power.*

Kill yourself! Suddenly the arm of the razor broke in half and the blade fell innocuously into the sink.

Steven looked at the broken plastic and noticed drops of blood covering the handle. Immediately, a piercing pain shot up his arm. The broken razor had pierced his finger leaving an ugly open wound. Quickly, he grabbed a hand towel, folded it tightly around his injured digit and sat on the edge of his bed. The pain from his wound had stifled the voice in his head. He felt calm and his body relaxed as endorphins coursed their way through his bloodstream slowly bringing him back from the slough of despair which had enveloped him.

28

Several days later and slightly inebriated from an afternoon's drinking session, but fully recovered from his bout of depression, Steven accidentally bumped into the girl he so admired, outside the university library.

"I'm so sorry. I wasn't looking!"

Steven scrambled on the floor picking up several books that he had knocked out of Anna's hands.

"Never mind," smiled Anna. "Accidents happen."

Steven looked at the books and sheepishly handed them to their owner.

"Coastal Geomorphology."

"Yes."

"Are you studying Geography?" enquired Steven timidly.

"Yes. it's my first year here. I'm on exchange from the University of Amsterdam."

He stared at Anna. His heart pulsated fast and a strange feeling coursed through his body creating sensations he had never felt before. Anna excited him more than anyone he had met and slept with in his entire life.

"My name is Anna."

"Steven. Steven Winwick, glad to meet you."

Steven extended his hand to Anna and she reciprocated by gently wrapping her fingers around his. Instantly an electrical charge raced through both their bodies as if being hit by lightning. Steven stepped backwards, still holding her hand, and let out a short gasp. Anna smiled, extricated her hand from Stevens and rubbed it gently.

"Are you okay?" he asked.

"That's not happened to me before," smiled Anna as she blushed with embarrassment. "I was just about to get some coffee would you like to join me?"

He didn't need any other persuasion and walked alongside Anna until they reached her room in Lloyd Thomas Hall.

"I think you could do with a coffee. Do English boys always drink alcohol during the day?" joked Anna. "Take a seat I'll be back in a minute."

He watched as Anna walked to the sink to pour some water into a kettle she was holding and noticed Mordillo posters covering the walls indicating Annas sense of humour. Sitting on her neatly made bed, he gazed at Anna's family photographs which lay on a small dressing table.

"Why is this man's head scribbled over in blue ink?" He asked picking up a picture of a group of businessmen some of whom were sitting and some of whom were standing to attention.

"I thought you'd be intrigued by that. Don't ask me why my father has defaced the man. I've asked him year on year, but he wouldn't tell me."

"That's curious. Sorry I wasn't being nosy."

"Of course not."

Steven took his coffee and looked intently at Anna who rested herself against the bedstead.

"Didn't I see you in the café weeks ago with your friends?"

Steven blushed.

"Yes. Chris and Sean. They're my best friends."

Anna took a sip of her coffee.

"Have you made any friends yet?" he said putting the cup down onto the floor.

"Not really. You're the first person I've really talked to. Most students have already made their friendship groups."

"Don't worry. Someone like you will soon make lots of friends."

It was Anna's turn to feel embarrassed as she smiled and flicked her hair back over her shoulders. She was just about to continue the conversation when there was a loud knock on the door. She rose and opened the door and saw Porter Owen standing in front of her.

"Oh, hello my lovely. I didn't know you had company. I've got something for you," he said and handed a note to Anna.

After quickly reading the contents of the note Anna looked at Steven and exclaimed, "It's from my father. I've got to go and see him. Its urgent. Sorry. Can we catch up another time?"

29

Two weeks later, and after meeting each other every day, Anna and Steven strolled up the one mile, serpentine, single track path which led to the resplendent Falcondale hotel. Whilst enjoying the scenery Steven couldn't help but remember that ten months earlier, when he and his new university friends had trodden the same route on the way for a freshers' party, the path was immaculately clean and devoid of wild flowers but now the borders of the path were riddled with Wandering Jew weed, Pigweed and Crabgrass.

"Penny for your thoughts?"

Steven stopped in his tracks, pulled Anna closer to him and gently kissed her on the lips.

"Nothing, just a bit nervous meeting you mum and dad for the first time."

Anna pulled Steven closer to herself and peered into his almond eyes.

"Don't worry. They just want to meet the man who has swept their beloved daughter off her feet."

After they had walked past a variety of coach houses and workers' cottages, they turned around a corner and Steven spotted the lime-lined driveway, adorned with pink and blue begonias, silver mounds and marigolds, which led to the imposing, white Italian villa- styled building which was Falcondale Hotel.

Nearing the hotel itself, he noticed how the walled gardens and hotel grounds looked across pastures, rising in gentle folds, to forest-cloaked hills. Although the hotel and its estate seemed to be immaculate Steven, on closer attention, saw that the eaves of the building and window frames were rotten in parts and some of the walls had hairline cracks with paint peeling off the masonry. Furthermore, he detected innumerable dandelions, chickweed and bull thistles infesting the perimeter of the building ruining the ambience of the edifice.

"There they are," Anna exclaimed as she pointed to her parents waving at them from inside the hotel restaurant.

As the young couple entered the building, walking past the oak-laden reception, they were greeted by a concierge who led them to the dining room. Seated by the window were Anna's parents. Steven watched as Anna escaped from his hand and rushed into the arms of her father.

"Mother. Father. This is Steven."

Anna's mother beamed a smile towards him whilst Anna's father held out his hand in anticipation of a handshake.

"So, you are Steven," Anna's father said. "I've heard so many positive things about you. I'm sorry we didn't meet you before, but we have been sightseeing around Wales...please sit. I hope you don't mind but I've already ordered for us...is that all right with you?"

Steven nodded in acknowledgement but as he was about to sit down, he accidentally knocked the dining table with his knee causing cutlery to crash onto the floor. As he bent down to pick up the knife and fork, his gold chain and St. Christopher pendant fell loose around his chin. Anna's father stared for what seemed an eternity at the jewellery and as he did so, his pallor changed. Sweat started to dribble down his immaculate brylcreamed hair and a slight twitch at the edge of his mouth was noticeable by all around the table.

"Darling are you okay?" quizzed his worried wife.

Anna's father looked up from Steven, took a folded, yellow-stained handkerchief from his trouser pocket and wiped his forehead.

"Please don't worry. I think an aperitif went down the wrong tube. Excuse me for a minute will you,"

He alighted from the table and headed towards the male restroom.

"Should I go and see if he is okay?" enquired a concerned Steven.

"Thank-you for your offer of help," replied Anna's mother. "My husband never accepts help from anyone. Isn't that right darling?"

"Yes. He's very independent indeed," agreed Anna.

Several minutes later Anna's father arrived back at the table and sat down without looking at Steven.

"Your origins Steven? Where you born in Liverpool?"

"Father," interrupted Anna. "I told you that Steven was born in Georgetown, British Guiana."

"So you did my darling," he replied sipping a glass of Beaujolais. "That's right your father was English and your mother Guianese Indian. Is that correct?"

Steven nodded.

"What a small world we live in. Did Anna tell you that I was stationed in British Guiana with my wife in the 1950s?"

"Yes. She did," Steven acknowledged. "Did you by any chance meet my father and mother? I know Guiana is a big country, but you might have met them at some point in time."

Anna's father took another sip of wine and evaded Steven's eyes.

"Do you have any photographs of your parents?" he enquired.

"Yes." Steven pulled his wallet from his pocket and took out a folded black and white photograph and handed it to him.

Anna's father unfolded the photograph and perused the faces of Steven's parents. Several seconds went by before he showed the photograph to his wife who without a word, scanned the images and then studied Steven's face. Still silent, but now with trembling fingers, Anna's father handed the photograph back to Steven and took another glass of wine and drank it as if trying to compose himself.

"A handsome man and a beautiful woman. I now know where you get your looks from," Anna's father said forcing a smile as he did so. "Unfortunately, our paths never crossed."

Steven looked at Anna's mother and noticed that her demeanour had also changed after studying the photograph. She too had finished her wine and started to fidget with the base of her glass.

After a minute or two of silence Anna's father asked, "I wonder if anyone would mind if we missed the next course. I would like to return to my hotel. I think I may need to take one of my pills. Unfortunately, I forgot to bring them with me."

"Are you sure you will be okay father?" implored Anna.

"Yes, Yes darling. Please don't fuss. We will see you tomorrow before we fly back to Amsterdam. Enjoy the rest of your meal."

As he said so a waiter approached Steven and whispered in his ear. With raised eyebrows he excused himself from the table and followed the waiter. Walking out of the dining room he noticed a seemingly familiar, small dark- haired figure with her back towards him.

"Mother? Mother?"

The figure turned around and stared at him.

"What are you doing here? Is everything all right?"

Suddenly and without warning Beebi started crying inconsolably. Steven rushed to her and hugged her tightly.

"What's wrong mother? What's wrong?"

Beebi pulled a clean, paper handkerchief from her handbag and wiped the tears from her face.

"It's your father," Beebi cried. "He's dead!"

The two words from his mother's mouth echoed around his mind like Thor's hammer striking a cold anvil. He began to feel light- headed and grabbed hold of the reception counter to steady himself.

"How... how did he die? Was he ill? Did he suffer? What happened?"

Beebi took hold of her son's hands and paused for a minute. Looking deeply and sadly into his almond eyes she squeezed him gently.

"He killed himself, Steven. He killed himself!"

He stared at his mother in disbelief and stood motionless

with a myriad of thoughts criss-crossing his mind.

"Steven? Steven what's the matter? What's happened?"

Steven turned to see Anna and her parents standing behind him.

"It's my father...he's dead!"

Anna let out a stifled cry and grabbed hold of her boyfriend. Hugging him tightly she looked at the woman he was talking to and realised, without any need for help, that it was his mother. Holding her hand out to Beebi she whispered quietly that she was sorry for her loss and turned towards Steven. Beebi smiled for a moment but unwrapped her hand from Anna's when she noticed the couple standing behind her.

"Order a taxi and take your mum back to the campus," Anna suggested. "You both have a lot to talk about. I'll explain to my mother and father."

Anna turned and looked at her parents who stood like statues, ashen faced and clearly disturbed as if they had seen a ghost.

After an awkward silence, Anna's parents left the hotel abruptly without acknowledging either Beebi or Steven.

Watching Anna's father and mother leave the hotel lobby Steven could not help but think that there was a darker reason for their sudden departure.

"I'm not sure your dad likes me." he said.

"Don't be paranoid Steven. It's just that he felt unwell," she replied.

"But did you notice he refused eye contact with me when he left and didn't even offer his condolences to my mother directly." Steven said.

"I know he likes you. I can tell," Anna replied. "Don't worry about it. Once he feels better, we will meet him again and I'm sure both of will get on ...what's the saying? Like a house on fire. But look let's not worry about that now. Take your mother back to her hotel and I'll go and speak to my parents."

Steven looked at Anna and squeezed her hand lovingly but at the same time a dark foreboding crossed his mind.

30

Henfaes House was a small guest house on Lampeter High Street, just a two minutes' walk from the university campus. Frequented by tourist and families of students, it was also a well -known source of accommodation for students unable to secure a room on the actual university campus. Steven held his mother's trembling hand as they alighted the staircase to the second- floor bedroom.

"One of your porters...Porter Owen kindly booked me into this place after he heard of the news of your dad's death. He sang your praises."

Steven smiled and comforted his mother as tears began to well in her eye

"He's a lovely bloke and very helpful," replied Steven. "Do you have enough money to pay for the room? I can..."

Before Steven could finish his sentence Beebi placed two fingers on his lips.

"Don't you worry about money. Everything has been sorted...thanks for asking anyway."

Although accepting what his mother had said, he couldn't but help to think of the expense she had incurred for a taxi from Liverpool together with the cost of accommodation. Money was tight at home and he knew his parents had no savings whatsoever.

"When did dad die?" enquired Steven sympathetically.

"Two days ago," Beebi uttered through a waterfall of tears.

He pulled his mother towards him and cradled her.

"He hung himself. Steven. Oh dear. He hung himself. It's all my fault!"

The very thought of his father hanging himself sent shivers down his spine and he felt an uncontrollable urge to vomit. Releasing himself from his mother's grip he walked to the sink and poured himself a glass of water.

A few moments later the silence was broken by Beebi.

"I shouldn't have pestered him in trying to get another job to make ends meet, He wasn't the man he used to be, and I think he knew that."

Memories of his father transmogrifying from a huge, muscled, smiling man to one that was a shadow of his former self swirled in his mind. Indeed, the last image of his father bidding him farewell from the station was testimony of his fall from grace.

"It's not your fault. Don't think that," murmured Steven caressing his mother's greying, black hair. "He must have had mental health issue and should have talked to someone!"

Steven knew he was right. His father had never, to his recollection, spoken about anything personal. Emotional literacy was not his forte and, as such, Steven reckoned that inability to express feelings was a contributory factor in his death.

"The funeral is next week," his mother said. "Will you come home with me tomorrow? The bus leaves at one o'clock or do you want to come later in the week?"

'Of course, I'll come home with you tomorrow!"

31

The next day, after breakfast, Steven walked through the Old Building and ran towards Anna's room, in Lloyd Thomas Hall, to let her know of his impending plans.

"Hey gorgeous are you up?" shouted Steven as he tapped on Anna's window.

After a few seconds without any answer he walked into the building and into her corridor. As he was about to knock on her door, Anna's neighbour, Sally, opened her door and looked at him.

"I bet she's fast asleep." said Steven.

"No, Steven," Sally replied sadly. "Didn't she tell you?"

"Tell me what?"

"She's flying back to Amsterdam with her parents today."

The colour from his face drained like a thermometer immersed in freezing cold water. Without saying another word to Sally he turned and ran out into the fresh air.

Leaning against the wall numerous dark thoughts invaded hismind. What was happening? Why was Anna going back to Amsterdam? Why didn't she tell him? Why couldn't she wait until he had sorted out his trip back to Liverpool for the funeral? Did her father dislike him? What was he going to do? What was he going to do?

"Hey Stevie boy are you ok? You don't look well?"

Through his blurred vision Steven could just about decipher the imposing figure of Carlos, the American exchange student.

Suddenly, Steven's stomach began to palpitate, and acid started to percolate upwards into his windpipe. Without further warning Steven began to wretch and the remnants of his breakfast peppered the pavement. About to fall to the ground Carlos caught Steven and rested him against the wall.

"Man! You are in right state. Let me take you back to your room."

32

Standing at his father's graveside, inside Anfield cemetery, Liverpool, Steven looked around at his fellow mourners. Less than twenty family and friends had congregated on the unusually cool summer's day to witness the final farewell of his father, George Winwick. It was noticeable to his mother that, unlike in British Guiana where her husband was once the beating heart and soul of the ex -patriot community, here in England George had been a mere abstraction, a man devoid of any real, true friends and a family member who had barely kept in touch with his brothers, sisters and cousins. As she threw pieces of dry, brown earth onto the wooden coffin, a large, cumulus-nimbus cloud slid, slowly, across the face of the sun blackening the sky. A slight, chill breeze accompanied the sudden darkness and meandered around the crowd of funeral-goers causing a few of them to pull their black coats closer to themselves in order to preserve some warmth. Steven held his mother's cold hand as she finished scattering the earth and watched as tears streamed down her face.

Back at his parents' home, the family members who had decided to stay for the wake solemnly chatted to each other whilst indulging in home-made spam and chicken sandwiches, bottles of wine and Mr. Kipling's cakes. Beebi rested on the armchair she had sat on for the past seventeen years attended by her favourite and closest relative, George's cousin, Bernice. Looking at his mother, Steven could not help but think that she was listening but not hearing. Her eyes betrayed a lack of interest in whatever condolences her friend was conveying to her. It was if she was watching a film that no one else could see, lost in each scene that was playing in front of herself.

"Time is a healer."

Steven diverted his gaze from his mother to the person who had just placed his large arm around his shoulders.

"Yes, your mother will overcome this loss. We all do."

He looked at his Uncle Charles, his father's brother. The only similarity between the two brothers was their height and the Winwick's unmistakable equine nose. Charles was a portly, ruddy-faced man with a crop of ginger hair and unkempt ginger beard and was the complete opposite, character wise, to George in every way conceivable.

"I know we've never been a close family, Steven but I'll make sure your mum will be taken care off," he said taking a large sip of wine. "Your father was a good man. A hardworking man. I was surprised he decided to return to Liverpool. He was doing so well in British Guiana until...."

"Come on Charlie, come and say your respects to Beebi!"

Arthur, George's youngest brother, took Charles by the arm and led him over to where Beebi and Bernice sat and then returned to his nephew,

"What did Uncle Charles mean?" asked Steven.

Arthur was the spitting image, facially, of George but fifteen years younger and at least three inches smaller. Steven had always liked him because he was one of the few relatives who would visit his father regularly and who would provide annual birthday and Christmas presents. Furthermore, Arthur's son, Christopher, who was only a few years older than Steven, had forged a friendship with him which had maintained to the present day.

"Christopher sends his regards. Unfortunately, he couldn't be here because of his exams in New York State University."

"I understand," replied Steven. "He rang me yesterday. But what was Uncle Charles going to say?"

Arthur pierced his lips.

"Didn't your father ever tell you why he brought you and your mother back to Liverpool?"

Steven shrugged his shoulders.

"In the fifties, all over the world, a white man marrying a black woman was frowned upon," stated Arthur. "Your dad had a great job as an overseer with Bookers plantation and we all thought he'd end up as manager especially as his Uncle Cecil was already there and a senior manager in the commercial side of the company."

Steven looked dumbstruck at his uncle, not only because he was unaware that his father held such a high position but also, more worryingly, he never knew his father had an uncle working for the same company.

Sensing what he was saying to his nephew was indeed a revelation, Arthur contemplated whether to reveal more of George's history for fear of opening a hornet's nest. However, he realised his version of events would be more palatable to Steven than the one Charles potentially would reveal.

"Your father was put under a lot of pressure not only from the owners of Bookers but also his uncle."

"What do you mean?" enquired Steven leading his uncle to the vestibule which was devoid of mourners.

"Well as I have said, in those days white men could consort with black women but they weren't allowed to marry them. That was against all the rules and conventions of the time."

"But what did his uncle do?"

"Your dad's father was meant to go to British Guiana at the beginning of the 1920's but he met his future wife and decided to stay in Liverpool and work as a boilermaker. His brother, Cecil, took his employment ticket and sailed over to British Guiana and after twenty years had worked himself up to the position of senior manager."

"Why did my father go to British Guiana?"

"Well this is the sad part," Arthur continued. "I know that you know that your dad was a war hero....so much so in fact that he was asked to become a warrant officer after World War Two had ended. Well, he was going to accept the promotion and all the privileges that come with it, when he received a telegram from his Uncle Cecil."

"What did the telegram say?"

"In short Cecil offered your dad an opportunity of a lifetime."

"What opportunity?" implored Steven.

"You have to remember Steven it was a long time ago....and society acted far differently from how it acts now. Cecil was married but childless. He had always liked your father, although his wife was not so keen! I don't think she liked anybody including her husband come to think of it."

Arthur put his arm around his nephew's shoulder and looked deeply into his eyes.

"As the eldest boy in the family, Cecil promised George not only his estate in British Guiana but also his estate in Fazakerley, Liverpool together with an agreement that your father would become a manager within eight years."

"So, my father went to British Guiana for the money?"

"Not necessarily Steven! Your dad loved Cecil but more importantly, after serving in the army all over the world, he had caught the bug for travelling abroad and immersing himself in different cultures. His yearning for travel started from school and if it was not for the outbreak of the war he would have gone to university as he had secured a scholarship to study Anthropology and History."

Steven stood dumbfounded. He had never heard this part of his father's history although he did know that his Uncle Charles lived in Fazakerley, in a detached bungalow, with three acres of land containing a tennis court and sailing boat.

"Anyway, when your dad started seeing your mum and even when Beebi gave birth to you, Cecil was convinced your father would eventually marry a white woman. Well, Cecil didn't know how much your father was in love with your mother and moreover what a principled man his nephew was! For years Cecil asked him to marry a white woman and even worse, Cecil's wife urged her husband to cut George out of their will unless your father agreed to do whatever they had asked. Deep down,

I'm sorry to say, Cecil's wife was a racist and poor Cecil was too weak to remonstrate against her."

"So, my father was disinherited because he married my mother?"

"I'm sorry to say, yes. When Cecil and his wife returned to England, they disowned your father, and on their deaths their whole estate was left to your Uncle Charles. George was cut out completely."

"But my father didn't mention this during his life and didn't seem to resent Uncle Charles. In fact, he only had good things to say about him."

"Well that's typical of your dad. He was a true gentleman with morals, courage and a sense of forgiveness. He told me that Charles was welcome to Cecil's estate. He personally wouldn't do anything different. He said he loved your mother deeply and no pound signs would ever separate him from her."

Pride and affection seeped into every pore of Steven's body at the thought that his father had sacrificed a fortune for love. But he wasn't all that surprised. He knew, deep down, his father was a kind, loving, charitable man who understood the true meaning of responsibility and honour. However, despite the feelings of love and pride pervading his body he felt utterly helpless and sad as he looked at his mother sitting lonely amongst her fellow mourners.

33

Steven alighted from the Aberystwyth to Lampeter coach, one week after the funeral and sauntered along the High Street in the direction of the university campus. As he was just about to cross the road, at the roundabout, a sudden mysterious urge made him glance in the direction of Conti's café. To his horror he spotted Alun sitting next to Anna in the bay window. He stared at the scene and as he did so, Alun caught his eye and, with a malevolent smile, he grabbed Anna by the neck and kissed her fully on her cheek. Upset and outraged Steven turned away abruptly and ran fast along College street, turning right into the campus grounds.

"Slow down boyo," shouted Porter Owen as Steven accidentally barged into him. "Where's the fire?"

"I'm, I'm sorry," replied Steven. "I can't stop."

"Anyway, good to see you back Steven...we've missed you."

Steven carried on running to his halls of residence as Porter Owen's words reverberated around his mind.

Locking the door behind him, he threw his belongings to the floor and gasped for air. Tears began to well in his eyes and a fury surged up from his abdomen setting alight a blazing rage in his mind. Suddenly, he turned and punched the wall, with all his force, leaving a knuckle imprint on the white plaster. Dark thoughts coursed through his mind. Was Alun going out with Anna? Why was she having coffee with him? Had she been seeing him before he left for the funeral? Did his friends know? He collapsed onto his bed and started crying uncontrollably.

"Steven, Steven!" the voice of Sean filtered through the locked door. "Porter Owen just told me that you were back. Can I come in?"

Steven fell silent biting his hand to stifle any cries he had been making. Lifting himself up, he tip-toed to the side of the door pretending not to be in. Waiting a few seconds, he peered underneath his window curtain and noticed Chris and Sean standing next to his door chatting with each other in earnest. After a minute or two, his friends knocked once more on his door, but without any answer, looked at each other, shrugged their shoulders and walked away in the direction of the Library. He rested his head against the wall and closed his eyes. What was happening? How would he cope with the death of his father, the sorrow of his mother and the loss of Anna? Breathing in deeply, he walked in front of the window and watched his friends disappear from view.

"Hey Paki!" Alun shouted in black contempt. "Anna tasted nice,,,didn't you know I was seeing her?"

Steven's world collapsed into a nothingness. Angry at being racially abused by the Welsh rugby player was nothing compared to being despondent at the thought that Anna was dating him. He stood transfixed as the pugnacious figure walked towards him across the manicured, green lawn.

"What are you going to do about it, Paki?" Alun continued to grin and scowl as he neared Steven's room in the Old Building. "Cat got your tongue or are you too much of a coward to do something about it?" he shouted.

Steven stared hatefully at his rival. Clenching his fists, he pushed his window open and glared at Alun.

"Why don't you step outside,,."

Suddenly, without warning and before Alun could finish his sentence Steven grabbed hold of his adversary's jumper and pulled him towards the window ledge. Using his karate skills, he performed a choke hold on his unsuspecting foe forcing him to gasp for breath.

"Mr.Winwick please let go of that poor young man! I hope you are not attempting to inflict any bodily harm on him. He certainly does not look well."

The mellifluous voice of Mr. Wigfield, Professor of Philosophy, floated into Steven's mind as if he was being hypnotized.

"Mr. Winwick!" continued Mr. Wigfield, in a quieter and more monotonous tone. "Let Mr. Lloyd go at once! His complexion doesn't quite match the orange and black of his rugby top. Does it now?"

Steven looked at the helpless face of Alun and then looked at Professor Wigfield. Slowly his grip loosened, and Alun slipped to the ground gasping for breath and rubbing his neck.

"I'm sorry Professor," murmured Steven looking at Alun writhing on the floor.

"I suggest Mr. Winwick, that in future you resolve your difference with talk not fists! That is the civilized thing to do. N'est pas? You have attended a few of my lectures to understand that debate and the pen is mightier than the sword and fists. Do I have your word that there will not be a repetition of these events?"

Steven nodded in embarrassment and anger.

"Very well. The matter ends here. Mr. Lloyd. I do not know what caused this vicious altercation, nor do I want to know. Please get up and refrain from embarking on any similar events in the future. Do you understand me? Otherwise I will have to inform the Senate!"

Professor Wigfield tapped his walking stick loudly on the quad stone floor, stared deeply into both Alun and Steven's eyes and continued his walk into the Old Building with the air of authority that becomes a respected professor.

Rising to his feet and clearly dazed, Alun glared menacingly at Steven.

"It's not over yet Paki!" he hissed threateningly. "I'll fuck you up one day!"

Steven smirked at Alun, closed his window, sat on the edge of his bed and trembled with intense anger and frustration.

34

The next morning Steven sat alone in Emlyn Evans café nursing a cup of black coffee.

"Here he is!" Sean said to Chris as they greeted their friend. "We've been looking for you since yesterday. We heard what happened to the fat Welsh git. Good for you."

Steven, blushed, nervously fidgeted with his cup and thanked his friends.

"Is he going out with Anna?" Steven asked not really wanting to hear the reply.

His friends remained silent and looked at one another, not daring to answer to the affirmative.

"Is he going out with Anna?" Steven repeated sipping his coffee.

"Anna arrived back a few days after you left for Liverpool. We've hardly seen her Steven," said Sean. "When I have seen her, she's looked lost and upset and tended to keep herself to herself."

"Alun said he was seeing her. Is that true?"

"Only at lectures I think," replied Chris. "I'm sure if you go and talk to her, she'll tell you."

Steven pondered the words for a moment, stood up and without a look at his friends exited the café.

Walking past the Library, heavy rain started to fall soaking Steven to the core. Cold, wet and frustrated he followed the path up to the quad, around the fountain and into the Old Building. As he strode past the chapel, a shiver crawled down his spine and he felt a dark foreboding. Once outside the building, heavy raindrops struck him like bullets hitting a target. Nevertheless, he steadfastly continued to Anna's room and noticed that the window was closed with the curtains drawn. Venturing into her corridor he knocked on her door and shouted her name.

After several attempts there was still no answer. Finally, Sally's door opened.

"Oh! Hello Steven! It's you. How are you? How is your mum?"

"Is Anna in?" Steven asked.

"She went to the refectory. If not there she must have gone to the library."

He knew that she was lying, He knew that something was amiss.

"But her curtains are drawn," he said quizzically.

"If she was in, I'm sure she would have answered. Sorry I don't know."

Sally watched as Steven left and as she closed her door, she smiled at Anna who was sitting close to the window with a worried look on her face.

"I think you should have spoken to him Anna, he looked distraught," Sally said holding Anna's hands in support and love. "He'll have to know sometime. It's not his or your fault for what's happened."

Anna looked at her friend and burst into tears.

"I can't. I can't. It would destroy him!"

"But Anna," Sally responded calmly. "If you tell him the facts, he'll understand that you were completely ignorant of events and you had no idea whatsoever of the secret."

Anna stood and looked at the figure of Steven trudging despondently back to the Old Building in the pouring rain. A sudden temptation to run after him and explain all, overcame her but the reality of the insidious predicament she was in crept back into her consciousness derailing the thin possibility of a reconciliation.

"I can't do it. I just can't. With university coming to an end in a few weeks' time, my parents pressurising me and making me feel guilty and Alun pestering me to go out with him I just need to be on my own to sort things out, otherwise I don't know what I may do to myself!"

35

Rain cascaded on Lampeter for three consecutive days. Steven usually loved the beauty this inclement weather brought to the surrounding green hills, lush meadows and flowing streams. However, with all that had happened recently his mood was as black as the thunder clouds that hovered ominously over the sleepy town. Every waking hour of the past few days had been excruciating for him. Thoughts of Anna and his father, good and bad, catapulted into his mind creating a canvas of memories which tormented him to the point of distraction. He seldom ate and ignored the constant requests of his friends to meet them in the union bar or at Emlyn Evans cafe. Such was his desire to be left alone he had sneaked out, at the dead of night and left messages with Porter Owen stating that he was too ill to see anyone and had been advised by the university doctor to stay indoors.

Feeling guilty at lying to his friends, he imbibed a glass of Thunderbird wine with several Anadin tablets, poured himself a hot bath and stepped into it wishing to wash away the depression enveloping him. Closing his eyes, he slipped deep under the bath water covering his body and face. Immediately a soft, dark voice from the back of his head started to commune with him. *Stay*

under the water and all your problems will disappear. The voice said. *That's it. Keep still. Don't move. Stay under the water. All will be better. Do not fight it. It will be all right.* The voice continued louder and louder and darkness began to seep into his mind until a distant memory of a swinging golden object appearing against a soft, brown background seemed to force the voice to subside and disappear. With a huge flailing movement, Steven forced his head out of the bathwater and inhaled the warm air surrounding him.

'Steven, Steven!"

Anna's shrill call from outside his room brought him back to his senses and created in him a sense of panic. He quickly stepped out of the bath, grabbed a towel and tip-toed to his front door.

"Steven. I know you are in there. Sean told me. Please open the door."

Anna stayed silent for a moment, anticipating a reply.

"Look. We have to talk...please open the door."

Steven put his hand on the latch ready to open the door, but quickly the dark voice roared back into his consciousness and commanded him not to open it. His hand dropped to his side and he listened intently.

"Steven. Please open the door. It's important. If I can just talk to you...to explain things!"

Don't listen to her. The dark voice instructed him.

"Please Steven," implored Anna. "We've only a few weeks before we all go back to our families. I can't face them without sorting this out. Please!"

After several minutes without any response to her pleadings, Anna turned and walked away listlessly. Steven listened as her footsteps disappeared into the evening and he slid to the floor sobbing.

Suddenly, a flurry of knocking emanated from the door again. He wiped his eyes with his bare arm and stood up waiting to hear Anna's voice again. Hope and joy had entered his heart once more revealing to him that he hadn't been abandoned by the love of his life. Waiting patiently to hear her voice, he gathered his thoughts and prepared himself to explain why he had been so evasive the past few days.

'Steven, boyo, I know you are in there," Steven's balloon of hope burst as the familiar voice of Porte Owen boomed through the door. "I've just seen that lovely girl of yours in tears by the library. Come on, boyo, you need to talk about what's troubling you."

Steven closed his eyes and dark despair invaded his mind once more. He had been abandoned. He had been let down by the one he loved so much. Now he was alone bereft of girlfriend, friends and family.

"Suit yourself, boyo. But if you change your mind you know where I am. By the way this letter came for you two days ago but you didn't bother to pick it out of your pigeon- hole. I'll slide it under the door."

Steven bent down and picked up the white envelope. Immediately he noticed a Liverpool postmark and his mother's neat handwriting. Turning the envelope around he realised, by its weight, that there was more than a letter inside. Slowly and carefully he lifted the seal to reveal blue-lined writing paper wrapped around two sepia-coloured photographs. Intrigued, Steven stood up and walked to his desk next to the window and sat down. He looked at the photographs. One photograph depicted a woman sitting against the backdrop of a waterfall. Unusually the face of the woman had been scribbled over with black ink. The second picture was an image of men wearing suits seated and standing, next to their wives and girlfriends. A board with the words, Booker Management 1955, written on it stood on the floor in the middle of the picture. Again, he noticed a woman seated in the centre of the front row, next to a man who must have been the Senior Manager, with her face also partially covered by ink. Without even reading the letter he immediately scoured in his desk for an ink eraser to discover what the women in the photographs looked like. After careful scrubbing, he flicked the tiny pieces of rubber, which had fallen off the eraser, onto the floor, revealing a beautiful, high cheek-boned woman, with fascinating eyes staring at him. When he had done the same to the office photograph Steven realised that the woman was the one and same person. Who and why had someone defaced the photographs? He placed the eraser in his trouser pocket and then looked more intently at all the people in the second picture. His eyes were drawn to one man in particular, standing in the back row who unlike everyone else in the photograph, stood side on to the photographer with his left arm resting on the shoulder of an Indian man with a wide grin stretched across his face. A cold shiver ran down his spine and the hairs on the back of his neck stood up. The man was his father. The muscled body, wide shoulders, shock of hair and equine nose were obvious trademarks of his father. He was stunned! He had never seen these photographs before, and he was fascinated by them. His eyes were drawn once again to the woman whose face had been angrily despoiled. There was something familiar about her, something inside his consciousness told him that he knew who she was. But who? Peering at the imposing gentleman sitting beside her, on her left, he again felt a connection. What that connection was, currently escaped him. Perplexed and thinking that the letter the photographs were wrapped in may shed light on the mystery he began to read his mother's writing.

"Dear Darling Steven,

I hope you are well and not dwelling, too much, on the death of your father. We both loved him. He is in a better place. He is at rest and all the evils of this world can no longer pierce his soul. So, my beloved son, just remember the happy times we had as a family. Allah has blessed us in so many ways that sometimes we forget the good times and only remember our trials and tribulations.

My son, this is a difficult letter for me to write. Please forgive me for not telling you this in person. I have agonised, all of my life, on whether or not I should reveal the truth to you...but your father's recent passing together with seeing Anna's parents has forced my hand. I couldn't bear to look into your eyes whilst telling you the truth so hence my letter.

Steven. I know you will have already looked at the photographs and knowing you as I do, I know that you would have cleaned the ink-stains from the face of the woman in the pictures. As you may have guessed I was the one who defaced the photographs. To my eternal shame, I thought the woman had conducted an affair with your father. Even though your father denied these accusations year after year, I still did not believe him...although I do now. Because of my raging jealousy I scribbled over her face ...I think it was my way of erasing her from not only my memory but also your fathers.

My dearest Steven what I am about to tell you is deeply personal and I am forever going to have hang my head in shame. When your father was sent, by Bookers, for management training in England for around a year I was brutally assaulted... I was sexually assaulted in British Guiana! You were but just a baby. At the time of the assault I didn't know who my attacker was. It was Khartoon, your aunty, who told me who my evil perpetrator was, as she had seen him running away from the scene some five minutes after the event. Nine months later I gave birth to a beautiful baby girl. No one ever suspected that I was pregnant. Anyway, after the birth of the baby I didn't know what to do. I was scared that your father would leave me. How was I going to bring up two children without any money? Luckily, Khartoon sorted things out for me. She went to the man who had raped me and threatened to expose him. I have no idea, whatsoever, how she convinced the man to agree to her terms. She never ever explained how he and his wife agreed to adopt Aisha, the name I gave to my baby, in return for not letting your father know what had happened. You may ask yourself why they agreed so easily to Khartoon's plan. I can only guess that the man's wife was unable to conceive and that as the baby was very light skinned no one would suspect the baby was adopted. I did not want to give my Aisha away but what could I do? You must believe me Steven. To my eternal shame I agreed to that plan and I have been living a lie ever since until I met Anna's parents in Lampeter. The man who raped me, Steven was Anna's father..."

On reading his mother's words Steven dropped the letter onto the floor and let out a primeval scream. The ramifications of the revelation were unbearable for him. He had fallen in love with his own stepsister! The very thought of the unethical situation made him feel incredibly nauseous and he ran to the sink and vomited.

Slightly relieved, but clearly shocked and dumbstruck, he picked up the letter and continued reading.

"I recognised Mr. De Witt and his wife, Debbie, immediately. To me they hadn't changed at all. Yes, they have got older, like myself, but it was like travelling back in time when I saw them some weeks ago. But more heart breaking for me was seeing Aisha or Anna as she is called now. I could see and feel that she was my little Aisha, my baby that I gave away all those years ago. My heart was broken for a second time. I thought I would die when I saw her. I wanted to hug her. To love her. To let her love me... but I couldn't. So, I had to leave immediately, and I knew that I couldn't tell you until I had thought things through. Please forgive me Steven. Please, please forgive me. I will phone you, in a few days' time, when I have decided what to do.

Your loving Mother."

Steven sat mesmerized by what he had just read. His brain seemed unable to compute the contents of the letter and a myriad of thoughts and questions crisscrossed his mind plummeting him, once again, into a slough of despair.

36

Hours passed and the laughter and chatter of students milling around the quad after an evening out at the union bar awoke Steven from the deep sleep he had fallen into after reading his mother's controversial and emotional letter. He rose and stared at himself in the mirror. The face staring back at him was smiling like a grotesque devil. He gazed into his reflection's eyes and slowly his whole body seemed to become possessed with an evil presence. He looked again at the stranger facing him in the mirror. The more he stared the more his body temperature rose. Cortisol rampaged throughout his bloodstream forcing him to hold his head in abject pain. Suddenly the dark voice whispered. *Now it starts Now this will be Armageddon day! No turning back. This is a world you will die in! No use! No use! No use! It is irreversible. Don't stop now and change your mind. Where are your friends to turn you back from this path of destruction? Where? Where the hell are they? Where are they now? Your friends have deserted you as well as your god. Your god has forsaken you! He is a heartless, feckless absentee landlord. You will murder both of them! Yes, yes! One by one! You know what to do, don't you? Don't you!*

Steven stumbled backwards, awkwardly, onto his bed grasping his head with both hands. Eyes shut, he grimaced as red, hot pain shot around his mind like fireworks in the dark of night. Saliva bubbled from the corners of his mouth, his chest tightened, and his heart felt as if it was being ripped apart. He tried to scream for help, but the dark voice silenced him.

You're going to need your gloves, hooded jacket and revolver. That's all you will need. The holy trinity! That's it put them into your bag.

Then they will die. Especially her... the bitch! She thinks that just because she looks so angelic and beautiful that you can't see that she's really a she-devil, a basilisk, a gorgon...the illegitimate spawn of Beelzebub. You know that beautiful exterior of hers is merely a mask. God was Keats so, so wrong when he said truth is beauty, beauty truth, because she is a liar and ugliness incarnate. But no one can tell by just looking at her, can they? Can they? If only people knew that below that smooth olive skin of hers beats the blackened heart of a monster. A monster that will be removed from the face of this earth... from the face of the universe. Yes. Her time has come. You are her Nemesis and she will feel your wrath. She knew all the time, didn't she? Didn't she? But she didn't tell you! Her love is as corrupt, disgusting and degenerate like that of Electra. She couldn't tell you. What twaddle! What lies! Everyone knew, everyone but you. The one person she was supposed to have loved. You have been made to look like Yorick the fool on the hill. But no more, no more! The whore! You will end this play your way. Calm down. Breathe slowly...calm down ...calm down...breathe slowly. Listen to me. Wait till everyone has left the quad and then make your move.

Fifty-five minutes later, Steven grabbed his holdall bag and walked like an automaton into the cool, night air. He stood still. The quad was empty and silent. He waited for the dark voice's instructions. When he heard it, he turned left and proceeded along the quad's path through the wooden arched doorway and across the damp croquet lawn in the direction of Harford halls of residence which lay adjacent to the library.

Nearing the library, a group of students, known to Steven, shouted salutations but he, under orders from the dark voice in his head, ignored their greetings and continued, stealthily, on his walk of vengeance. As he did so he opened his bag, slipped his gloves on, placed his balaclava over his head and pulled out his revolver. The dark voice congratulated him on his actions. *You know it's too late to go back* it whispered soporifically. *Where are your friends now? Where? You have suffered enough. You are not to blame for what you are going to do. Conscience isn't going to make a coward of you. You have tried to forgive. Haven't you? You have tried to give them the benefit of the doubt. But they betrayed you. You have the right to do what you are going to do. You have the right. You have the right.*

"Why have you got that balaclava on?" Alun shouted, leaning on the Library wall holding a can of Foster's lager. "To hide your ugly face Paki?"

Alun's insults bypassed Steven's auditory cortex.

"Pretending to be deaf also? Come here. I've been waiting to kick your head in, Paki!"

Steven, hypnotized by his dark, internal voice, strode slowly towards his foe making eye contact all the way. Unnerved by Steven's black, brooding, intense stare and threatening posture Alun threw his can onto the floor and charged towards his opponent.

Now do it, the dark voice ordered Steven. *Do it! Do it! Do it now!*

As Alun swung a right hook, Steven continued forward and absorbed the punch but felt no pain. Alun, angered at the lack of impact his punch had registered, threw an upper cut squarely onto Steven's jaw but once again Steven stood unflinching and stared malevolently into his enemies' eyes. Alun, hypnotized by his gaze, stumbled back onto the library wall and as he did so Steven pointed his revolver at him.

Alun looked down at the metal object resting against his chest. Unable to offer any protestations his eyes widened in fear and he exhaled a loud gasp as Steven pulled the trigger of his revolver. Slowly Alun's lifeless body slid onto the ground leaving a vertical red line of blood against the white wall of the Library building.

Well done, well done the dark voice chuckled. *One down, one to go. See how it was so easy to eliminate one of your enemies. Now concentrate on the next one. Don't let anything get in your way. You know you have to do it. Don't you? Who does she think she is? Who? Who? Who? She is a whore, a deep ditch whore. Her treachery is unbelievable. Eve, Pandora, Agrippina, Irma Grese, Myra Hindley are indeed angels bathing in milk and honey compared to her. Do you think she is Rahab? Rahab who is to be saved? No, no do not even go there. She has no redeeming qualities. She is evil incarnate. No angels listen to her when she prays for forgiveness. They are ashamed of her. They are decreed by the Almighty to let her succumb to her fate alone and helpless. So be it. So be it. This will be an execution not a murder and all the innocents of the world will congratulate you. Yes. They will thank you for removing a cancer from this world.*

Steven slowly turned and walked back, through the empty quad, the silent Old Building, around the lonely Norman mound and into Anna's unlit corridor in Lloyd Thomas Hall. He stopped outside her room and knocked on the door. There was no answer. Suddenly a throng of laughter emanated from Sally's room. Steven listened and then knocked on the door once again. He gripped the revolver tightly in his hand and pushed the door. To his amazement the door opened. He stepped inside and switched the light on. The room was empty.

Close the door and wait for the whore, the dark voice commanded. *Then kill her. But take your time, enjoy yourself with her. You know what I mean. Don't you?*

Steven closed the door quietly behind him. He walked to Anna's bed and brushed the sheets with his hand. Then he opened her wardrobe, flicked through her dresses, and placed one of her blouses against his nose and inhaled deeply. After a minute or two he walked to her dressing table and noticed the photograph he had seen before, laid next to a clock radio. He lifted the photograph and studied the faces' and figures of the men staring back at him. They looked vaguely familiar. As he stared at the man whose face had been scribbled over in ink, he placed the revolver in his inside jacket pocket, then retrieved his eraser from his trouser pocket. Slowly and carefully he removed the ink from the photograph and blew the rubber shavings onto the dressing table. He shook the photograph to remove any other traces of rubber to reveal the face newly exposed to him. He let out a stifled gasp. Staring back at him was the smiling face of his father. He dropped the photograph onto the dressing table and as he did so, he noticed another photograph slipped into the top left-hand corner of the dressing table mirror. This photograph, he realised, was an exact copy of the one his mother had given him. Taking it from the mirror he looked at the woman seated in front of Kaieteur Falls and then turned it around and saw faint, faded writing on the back. Steven squinted and read the words, *remember not to touch small amphibians, love George.*

I told you she knew, shouted the dark voice. *I wasn't lying to you. This will make it all the easier. Won't it. Won't it.*

Suddenly the door opened, and he diverted his gaze to the figure standing in front of him.

"Steven, you scared me! What are you doing here? I didn't think you wanted to see me."

He looked at Anna and then at the photograph in his hand. He remained silent.

Anna walked forward and stopped a few feet from him.

"I'm glad you came. I've been so worried. I tried to see you so many times," Anna cried. "I even wrote you a letter to explain things."

Anna pointed to an unopened envelope on her dressing table. Steven looked at the envelope and then back at Anna. Heat started to permeate throughout his body and darkness forced itself into his mind. He stood motionless, his eyes narrowed, and he felt tingling in his fingers. Flashing lights illuminated his darkened mind and he began to perspire profusely.

"Steven. Are you all right? Do you need a glass of water?"

He could see Anna's lips move but heard nothing. He stood facing her transfixed as if he had been mesmerized by an expert hypnotist.

"Steven, sit down here!"

Anna touched his hand and immediately, as if he had been hit by a bolt of lightning, he regained his senses.

End it now. End it now! The dark voice screamed entering his consciousness once more. *This is the time. Time to eliminate the lying whore. Now. Do it now!*

Without thinking he struck Anna across her face sending her crashing onto the dressing table leaving her prone on the floor with her possessions scattered all around her.

Good. That's it. Now do her some more damage. Do it! snarled the dark voice, as Steven placed his knee firmly on her spine.

"Please Steven! Don't hurt me! What have I done?" Anna pleaded as blood trickled from her nose onto the floor and extreme pain shot up her spinal cord.

She knows what she did. She knows. Don't listen to her. Just finish her. Go on. Don't hesitate.

"Steven, please let me go. Why are you doing this to me? I love you. I've been trying to see you and explain what happened when my parents left."

Lies. Damned lies. Ignore what the whore is saying. The dark voice ordered. *Finish her!*

Anna twisted her body and extended her arm grabbing Steven's hand. The sudden touch of Anna sparked an involuntary response in his mind and for a few moments the dark voice melted away leaving him, calm and cool but immensely confused.

Looking at Anna trapped under his knee, he quickly stood up and lifted her to her feet.

"I'm sorry! I don't know why i...."

Staring at Anna's bloodied face his body started to cool down and his heart rate subside. Feelings of self- loathing, disgust, shame and dishonour permeated his very soul. What had he done?

"Just sit," whispered Anna guiding him to her bed. "Take a deep breath. You need a drink of water."

He closed his eyes but the dark voice ordered him to open them. Once done as instructed he saw Anna heading to the door of the room instead of the sink.

There. I told you. She's a cunning vixen. You can't trust her. She has a viper's tongue. She tells you one thing and does another. The whore. Put out her light. She is a harlot. Put out her light. Kill her not tomorrow but tonight!

"Why do you still lie to me?" screamed Steven as he lunged at Anna and dragged her back onto the floor. "Why?"

"Steven," Anna gasped. "I wanted to tell you everything. I only knew the facts when my parents told me back in our home, in Amsterdam. I wrote it all down when you refused to see me. Steven you have to believe me!"

"You could have phoned me. No. You are liar!"

Steven placed his arms around her neck and squeezed.

"Please Steven. Stop. Sto....."

That's it. Squeeze harder. Harder! Nearly there. Just a little bit more. A little bit more. Well done. It is finished!

Suddenly the dark voice flew out of his mind. He looked at his hands as they relaxed from under Anna's neck. He watched as the blood, which had drained from his fingers and palm, returned. He stood up and stared in horror at her limp body. Steven's heart raced and every pore of his body began to burn. Panic embraced him and without thinking he picked up the envelope which lay next to Anna and ran into the cool night air.

As he gasped for breath and rested against Lloyd Thomas's wall Steven's heartbeat doubled in pace. Perspiration ran down his temples and slowly a black veil drew across his mind.

After a few moments he looked up into the night sky and noticed the moon peering down at him.

Fear, shame, worry, horror and images of Anna raced through his mind as he suddenly took flight through the campus and raced along Station Terrace until he reached the foot of a hill next to the local lumberyard. Although the coolness of the night enveloped him, heat from his core burnt every inch of his body and white noise infiltrated his mind forcing him to grab hold of a metal gate, which led through to the hill, in order to prevent himself from collapsing to the floor with mental anguish. After several minutes, but still in intense pain, he opened the gate and ran headlong up the hill following the light of the moon. At the summit he placed his hands on his hips, bent double and took a huge intake of air. As he straightened up, he raised his head and saw the full moon glaring at him. Alone and desolate Steven looked down at the lifeless campus. Tears welled up in his eyes as flashbacks of his year at the university snapped quickly in and out of his mind's eye. Tormented by his memories, he collapsed onto the damp grass and he felt a crunching noise underneath him. Slowly he placed his hand into his jean's back pocket and pulled out Anna's crumpled letter.

He opened the envelope with trembling fingers and stared at her neat handwriting. With a deep, anguished breath he read,

"Darling Steven,

I know that if you are reading this letter you have refused to see me. Steven, why didn't you let me explain things in person? Why did you not meet me? I have been out of my mind with worry since the arrival of your mother. I'm sorry I left for Amsterdam without telling you, but I didn't have any option. My father insisted. He said he had something important to tell me and it needed to be said at home not Lampeter. Steven I also know from your friends that you have been upset because of Alun's interactions with myself. But believe me there is nothing between him or I. He follows me around like a lapdog and despite my protestations he keeps on trying to persuade me to go out with him. But please believe me Steven I love you not Alun. I have missed you so, so much...."

Steven wiped away the tears which streamed from his eyes and paused for breath as the moonlight shone on him.

"Steven before my family and I flew out to Amsterdam your mother came to see my father. I realise now that what was said between them was the reason why my father had insisted on me leaving straight away. Once I was at home, I persuaded my father to tell me everything. Steven I was shocked and ashamed at his answers. I'm sure, by now, that your mother would have told you the whole story. I couldn't believe my father could behave in the manner he did. I can't and will not condone his actions. My poor mother had to suffer his misdemeanours all of her life...she feels equally guilty and ashamed but at least she forced him to do the right thing. Steven I can't turn the clock back and save your mother from the awful deed my father did to her! I can only imagine the hurt and terror she must have felt not at only at the time of the incident but also when she came face to face with my father in Lampeter. But Steven you must forgive my mother! She was the one, together with Khartoon your mother's sister, who persuaded my father to legally adopt my and your half-sister Marie. Marie and I are very close and when she was told the news her world came crashing down also, but she is now beginning to come to terms that she has a half-brother in England... you!"

Steven dropped the letter onto the grass and confusion reigned in his consciousness. What he had just read seemed insane. His own mother had told him that Anna must be his half-sister. How could she be wrong? Could she be wrong? Steven re-read the sentences slowly and as he did so, he noticed a small, rectangle piece of plastic by his knee. He picked up the object and realised he was holding a photograph. Four smiling people, two teenage girls and a man and woman stared at him standing on a bridge over a canal. Steven recognised, immediately, Anna and her parents and then looked intently at the other girl in the photograph. Hairs all over his body rose as he stared at the mirror-image of himself. Long black hair, almond eyes, olive skin and high cheekbones the young girl had all the physical attributes which were shared between his mother and himself. His mother had been wrong after all!

'Steven, unfortunately your mother was not the only victim of my father's unwanted advances. I now know that I am also the product of a heinous sexual crime committed by him. Again Debbie, my adopted mother, accepted me as her own and both Marie and I have been brought up as twins. We have never known the truth of our birth until now. Steven, I want to tell you and your mother everything. I know it won't be easy but please Steven once you have read this maybe you will understand why I left and why I have tried to see you for the past few weeks. I know you must be feeling hurt and upset but I know we can sort things out. Please Steven get in touch soon.

Love and kisses,

Anna "

Steven crunched the letter in his hand and felt his heart break in two realising that he had murdered both Alun and Anna on hearsay, innuendo and misinformation. He collapsed onto his knees and stared silently at the moon. Slowly he pulled his revolver from his jacket pocket and placed it against his temple.

Go on do it, laughed the voice. *Finish it. You are the fool on the hill. You have nothing left. Don't be a coward. End it now!*

Steven put his finger on the trigger and closed his eyes slightly. Suddenly, he felt an icy chill run up his spine forcing his body to tremble involuntarily and his eyes to open. Clouds slowly drifted across the moon's face and as he stared sideways looking at the university, he saw his moonlit shadow slowly disappear.

Notes

"Erhalten Sie Weg! Erhalten Sie Weg! Erhalten Sie Weg" translated means "Get away."

'Mein Gott Du Indische liebhaber! Du bist ein Arsch" translated means "My God! You Indian lover! You are an asshole!"

"Big tree fall down, goat bite he leaf," translated means "When a great man falls, he is no longer feared and respected."

"If yuh eye nah see, yuh mouth nah must talk," translated means "You must see for yourself before you talk."

"Don't mind how bird vex, it can't vex with tree" translated means "It does not matter if you are annoyed with conditions at work, you have to return to your job." Similarly, although you may be frustrated with the situation in your homeland, you may still have to return to it.

"Letters of Hindu Indentured Laborers: Letters of Jaipal Chamar and his son Ayodhya Das Quoted in: Brinsley Samaroo: The Indian Connection: The influence of Indian Thought and Ideas on East Indians in the Caribbean. In *India in the Caribbean*. Edited by Dr. David Dabydeen and Dr. Brinsley Samaroo. 1987)

"Seven years nah too much fuh wash speck off ah bird neck," translated means "Some people will never change their ways and attitude."

"Du Sau. Ich werde meinem Mann von Ihren Anspielungen erzähle," translated means "You pig. I will tell my husband about your innuendoes.".

"Prynhawn da chi bastardiaid Saesneg" translated means "Good afternoon to you English bastards."

"Croeso yn ol Sean my Saesneg friend! And you, you chi hyll gyfunrywiol" translated means ""Welcome back my English friend Sean! And you, you ugly homosexual."

"Eistedd i lawr" translated means "sit down"

Printed in Great Britain
by Amazon

83605912R00109